Martha jumped when she heard a knock on the door.

Moses was standing in the doorway, and his jaw dropped open at the sight of her. "Martha! You look, *um*, great."

"Thank you, Moses." Martha was a little embarrassed, and so spoke formally. Her community was not in the habit of complimenting anyone, but she realized that Moses must be quite surprised to see her in *Englischer* clothes for the first time. "Come in."

Moses was still standing in the doorway. "I've never seen you in a dress before."

"But I've always worn dresses," she protested.

"Not like that." Moses's jaw was still hanging open. He walked in and Martha looked behind him.

"Where's your *mudder*?"

"She kept going. I'll get a taxi home." He handed the pie to Martha.

"*Denki, denki* so much." Martha smiled. "That was so good of you to come to my rescue."

"I'll always come to your rescue, Martha." Moses smiled at her, and her heart leaped in response.

"Stay for dinner," she said on impulse.

Ruth Hartzler is a *USA TODAY* and internationally bestselling author of clean and sweet romance, mystery and suspense, including Amish romance, Christian romance and Christian cozy mysteries. Ruth is the recipient of several All-Star Awards.

THE NARROW WAY

USA TODAY Bestselling Author

Ruth Hartzler

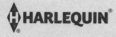

ISBN-13: 978-1-335-49974-5

The Narrow Way

First published in 2015 by Ruth Hartzler.
This edition published in 2020.

Copyright © 2015 by Ruth Hartzler

Recycling programs
for this product may
not exist in your area.

This edition published by arrangement with Harlequin Books S.A.

For questions and comments about the quality of this book, please contact us at CustomerService@Harlequin.com.

Harlequin Enterprises ULC
22 Adelaide St. West, 40th Floor
Toronto, Ontario M5H 4E3, Canada
www.Harlequin.com

Printed in U.S.A.

THE NARROW WAY

Chapter One

After a morning of goodbyes, tears, and shuffling boxes, Martha Miller tossed her new house keys on her bed and searched through the apartment. The space was large and bright, with two bedrooms, a kitchen, and a living area. There was plenty of room for all her treasures: even more when you considered that Martha had no treasures. After all, she was Amish.

With her footsteps echoing over the polished wooden floors, Martha moved to the refrigerator in search of a celebratory lunch. She found a block of moldy cheese and half a can of whipped cream, and though the meal was a far cry from the lemonade and meat pies of her childhood celebrations, Martha sat on the floor and nibbled the edges of the cheese, feeling the stir of adventure in her heart.

Her housemate, Sheryl Garner, an *Englischer* who took the second and far larger bedroom, was working the whole afternoon. On the four occasions they had met, Sheryl struck Martha as a nice, although softly rebellious, *Englischer* girl. She had short hair that was pink on the ends, a nose ring, and lipstick so bright it would put the sun to shame.

Sheryl had given Martha the keys that morning and told her to get comfortable. She had also mentioned that tomorrow they would go shopping. Martha stopped nibbling on the cheese and looked down at her plain dress. She could wear the clothes of an *Englischer* now, the jeans and the shirts with the funny slogans, and although she felt a childlike glee at the very idea, she would miss the security of her simple dresses, her prayer *kapp* and bonnet, and her woolen cloak. She wondered what she might buy with the money stashed in the bottom of her purse.

Martha wanted to have a chocolate business, and she had started by selling her treats at the local farmers' markets. She had made enough from the venture to live in this strange new world for two months, although she really needed to find a job as soon as possible. Now she wondered who might take an Amish girl with little experience in jobs common with the *Englisch*. She was a very good cook, having taken after her talented mother in that department, although jobs like that were likely hard to find, and she was not qualified for anything else. Martha sighed. She was so busy thinking on the clothes, the chocolate business, and her job, that it was a second before she realized someone was opening a window in the living room.

Martha froze as she listened to the person climb

through the window, land on the floor, and start to move through the living room, only to collide with the sofa and fill the air with a string of curses. From her spot on the floor near the fridge, she could not see if it was her new housemate, although Martha suspected that Sheryl would use the front door. Panic set into her heart and sweat dappled her forehead.

"Anyone home?" The stranger's voice, a *mann's*, and very deep, echoed through the apartment. "I'm just grabbing the cups I left here last weekend, and then I'll get out of your hair."

Martha furrowed her brow. Did she have time to scuttle back to her bedroom, lock the door, and hide until the *mann* left? Before she had time to consider the idea properly, the *mann* stepped into the kitchen. He was young, with dark hair and large brown eyes, ripped jeans, and a shirt emblazoned with a guitar. Martha swallowed.

"You're not Sheryl." The *mann* stared down at the strange girl eating moldy cheese on the kitchen floor. "Unless you are Sheryl, and I'm still extremely drunk."

"*Nee*. No, I'm Martha."

"Hello, Martha the mouse," he replied, holding out a hand. Although she hesitated for a moment, unsure about touching the hand of a strange *Englischer* boy, she relented and allowed him to help her off the floor. "I'm Gary. Sorry if I gave you a fright. I just live upstairs. Sheryl and I are friends. How long have you known her?"

"Not long." Martha quickly placed the cheese back

in the fridge. The thought of anyone, let alone a young man with tousled hair and sleepy eyes, catching her sitting on the floor and eating made her shiver. "I'm renting the second room. This is actually my first day here. I only just now moved in."

"I know," said Gary, a lopsided grin spreading over his handsome face. "I'd have remembered you. Do you want me to grab some food from my apartment, or do mice only eat cheese?"

Half an hour later, Martha sat across from Gary. On the table between them sat bowls of colorful Fruit Loops, toast, jam, scrambled eggs, and cups of orange juice. Martha had never eaten Fruit Loops before, and she felt her heart beating out a rhythm as the sugar roared through her system, although that might have been caused by the disheveled boy sitting across from her.

"So what's the go, Martha? What do you do?" asked Gary, buttering his toast.

"I want to start a chocolate business. What about you?"

"Right on," he said, looking up from his toast and grinning. "Myself? I'm in a band. I play the drums. We've got a real different sound you know. It's authentic. Nobody's in it for the fame or glory, man. It's all about the music."

Martha was struck by how different *Englisch* and Amish boys were. Sun filtered through the windows, throwing a halo of yellow light around the pale Gary. The boys she had grown up with, like the Hostetler *bruders*, worked on the farm with their father as soon as they were grown, their bodies browning in the sun. Martha's good friend, Moses Hostetler, the third oldest of the brothers, would make Gary look like a ghost. Martha's mind drifted to wonder what Moses was doing at this exact moment.

"What are you doing?" she asked suddenly, watching Gary cut his slices of toast into triangles.

"Cutting toast?"

"But why don't you cut it straight down the center?"

"Because I'm a rebel. You should check me out," Gary added, his mouth full of toast. "My band, I mean. You might like what you see." Then he glanced at his watch, slammed his fist on the table, and said, "Damn it. I'm late."

As he moved toward the window, Martha picked up the glass that Gary had toppled over and cried, "But what about all this food?"

"You keep it, little mouse." Gary flung one leg over the windowsill and pulled himself onto the fire escape. Then he ducked his head back into the apartment. "I wouldn't want you to disappear before we've had a chance to get to know each other," he said with a wink, vanishing into the golden sunshine.

Martha sat once more, wondering if all *Englisch* boys climbed through windows and lived on Fruit Loops, or if Gary was just as unique among them as he would be among the bronzed bodies of the Hostetler brothers. For the first time in her life, the world was not full of chores and dust, but fresh and full of curiosities. Martha picked up a new slice of bread, and cut it into triangles.

Chapter Two

Martha paused outside the café, staring at the hand-written *Help Wanted* sign in the window.

> *Help Wanted!*
> *Short order cook to start immediately.*
> *Must be well presented, qualified, and experienced.*
> *Apply within.*
> *No timewasters need apply.*

Martha could barely contain herself with excitement: here, finally, a job she could apply for. She was an excellent cook, used to preparing large amounts of food. She was well qualified, to be sure, and most certainly experienced, with all the cooking she had done for as long as she could remember.

Martha peered through the windows, trying to get a sense of the café. It appeared small, and the tables and chairs were all of wood. There were metal stools alongside a bar for the coffees. Martha's heart at once sank. *I'm not a barista*, she thought, chewing her lip. Still, the advertisement had not mentioned barista duties, so Martha thought there would be no harm in applying. What was the worst that could happen?

And so, with a deep breath to steady her nerves, and a silent prayer to *Gott* to ask for His blessing, Martha walked out of the bright sunlight and into the dim brown and green interior of the little café. A barista pointed her in the direction of a door at the back of the café, but as soon as she reached it, a smiling and plump woman burst out carrying two plates of omelets, which she at once handed over to the waitress and then looked up at Martha.

"I'm here about the job," Martha said, noticing the woman's eyes light up at her words.

"Come with me."

The woman ushered Martha into a back room that appeared to double as a store room and a little office. "I'm Ava, and my husband, Logan, and I run this store. Our cook didn't show up for work this morning and we just found out that she's getting a divorce and moving interstate." Ava sighed. "We had no idea, so it's caused us quite some trouble. You're qualified and experienced?"

Martha nodded.

Ava clasped her hands together in delight. "It's mornings only, Monday through Friday. Can you start at once?"

Martha nodded again. "Yes, I can start right now.

I can't make coffee though," she said, worried about the consequences of that admission.

Ava waved her hand at her. "No matter, we have baristas. It's a morning cook we don't have now. I need a cook, not a barista or a waitress. Now, we do breakfasts and lunches: sandwiches, pancakes, crepes, Belgian waffles, eggs, omelets. Oh, can you do chicken corn chowder soup? What about creamed chipped beef or scrapple?"

"Oh, yes, I do those all the time," Martha said.

Ava beamed, and continued. "We also go through a lot of cakes and pies, and we have a strong, passing tourist trade. Are you experienced with red velvet cake, pumpkin pie, apple dumplings, whoopie pies, and shoo-fly pies?"

"Yes, I make them all the time," Martha said, sending a quick prayer of thanks to *Gott* for finding her what seemed like the ideal position. *And Sheryl had said that a job would be almost impossible to find*, she thought.

Ava stood up and rustled through a filing cabinet. "All right then. I'll give you a trial. Like I said, five mornings a week, weekdays only. Start is seven thirty in the morning promptly, and end is at one thirty in the afternoon. Here's a slip of paper with rates of pay, and fill out this form"—she deposited the form and a pen in front of Martha—"and then I'll give you an apron, unless you want to go home and change and then come back?"

Martha looked down at her plain black pants and matching black blouse that Sheryl had insisted she borrow to wear for job searching. "No, that will be fine. I'll start now."

Ava nodded. "Excellent."

Martha could scarcely believe her luck, although it wasn't luck, she reminded herself, but a blessing from *Gott*. Not only that, but her apartment was only a short walk from the café. *Gott* had truly blessed her.

After her first day at work, Martha hurried home, excited that Ava seemed pleased with her on her very first day in an actual job. She wished she could tell her *daed*, her *mudder,* and her *schweschders*, but for now her new roommate, Sheryl, would have to do. Martha approached the apartment building, thinking it was nothing like any building she was used to, with so many people living so closely together, and none of them related to each other. The old building looked somewhat tired and worn from the front, with peeling paint on the cream timber walls, but the brightly colored flower gardens certainly gave the place a cheerful appearance.

Martha was surprised that she was able to afford a room here, even a small second bedroom in a renovated apartment, which likely originally had one large master bedroom and was renovated for the rental market, or so she suspected. Her bedroom was tiny, but Martha was thrilled that she had finally managed to find cheap accommodation. Sheryl said that Martha had been the only suitable person to answer the newspaper advertisement, although Martha couldn't see how that was possible. Still, she was grateful, and this new job meant that her worries were now over.

She would be able to work on her chocolate business at weekends, and even afford to set it up, at least in small stages. Plus, Sheryl seemed nice, although they couldn't be more different. Besides her bright hair, Sheryl always wore a great deal of makeup, short skirts, and had an awful lot of jewelry hanging off her.

When Martha hurried through the door and told Sheryl the happy news about her new job, Sheryl's mouth fell open. "To tell you the truth, I didn't think you'd be able to find anywhere to take you on. So, what, you're doing the cooking?"

"Yes." Martha beamed. "I don't have to make coffee, serve tables, or anything, just cook."

Sheryl nodded her approval. "That's amazing, well done. I'm surprised though, with you not qualified for anything."

Martha was puzzled. "But I'm qualified for cooking."

"You are?" Sheryl raised her eyebrows. "You have a certificate or something?"

Martha bit her lip. "Um, no, but I've done a lot of cooking for as long as I can remember."

Sheryl shrugged and handed Martha a mug of coffee. "Come and sit down. I don't mean to be a wet blanket or anything. I suppose they didn't ask for qualifications?"

Martha felt sick to the stomach. "The advertisement in the window said they wanted someone experienced and qualified, as far as I can remember." She sat down in the comfortable sofa opposite Sheryl.

"That means that they wanted you to have a certificate," Sheryl explained slowly.

Martha's hand flew to her mouth. "Oh, I had no idea! What have I done?"

Sheryl waved her hands at her. "Look, don't worry about it. If they didn't ask to see any qualifications, they won't worry. Besides, you said they were desperate. So long as they're happy with your work, I don't think they'll care."

Martha sipped her coffee and thought for a moment. "I'll have to tell them I don't have qualifications, though."

"Are you mad?" Sheryl's voice rose in horror. "You can't! You won't have a job if you do that. The main thing is that they're happy with your work. It's not being dishonest. Just don't tell them, and hope they don't ask to see any certificate or anything."

Martha nodded, and settled down to watch television with Sheryl. Her stomach was churning and her discomfort was due to several reasons. She felt she was in fact being dishonest for not declaring the fact to her employers that she had no qualifications. She had no idea that they meant a certificate when she applied, but she did know now. She also was not comfortable watching so much television with Sheryl. Martha had been brought up to be busy every minute of the day, and sitting down doing nothing made her uneasy. Television had been a big novelty for the first few days, but now it just seemed a complete waste of time.

The reality of the *Englisch* world was just starting

to sink in. On the one hand, it was different and exciting, but on the other hand, the *Englischers* seemed
to waste a lot of time. On the downside, there was
no community help or support. There was no going
down to the barn to collect eggs or to milk the goat;
one went to a store and bought such items. Sheryl
certainly did not make her own clothes, and seemed
to own more clothes than Martha had seen collec-
tively in her lifetime. For her dinner, Sheryl always
put packets of food in a microwave and they were
cooked incredibly quickly. Martha did not think she
would ever be able to use the microwave, although
she had adapted quickly to the electric oven.

Martha closed her eyes tightly during a particularly violent scene in *Game of Thrones* and sighed
aloud. *The* Englischers *sure are funny*, she thought.
*They are in such a hurry all the time, but then they
sit down for hours and watch TV and do nothing.*

Chapter Three

Martha jumped out of the taxi and smiled widely when she arrived at the Millers' house. It was amazing how she felt right at home there. Then again, it had been her home all her life, but she also felt at home in the *Englisch* world. Martha wondered if everyone who had been on *rumspringa* felt this way. She supposed most did.

Martha paid the taxi driver, but before she could walk to the house, a buggy came into view. She waited to see who it was.

She recognized David Yoder driving. With him was Mary, and his sister Jessie. Jessie's expression was sullen, but that was normal for Jessie, Martha figured. Jessie had done her best to stop Jacob Hostetler marrying Martha's sister, Esther, but now Jacob and Esther were married and expecting a *boppli*. Jessie had a reputation as a troublemaker. On the other hand, Mary was a delight. The bishop had sent Mary to help Mrs. Miller after the buggy accident, and she had stayed on in the community.

Mary wasted no time getting out of the buggy. "Martha!" she shrieked, running over to her. For a moment Martha thought Mary would envelop her in a large hug, but she restrained herself. "I've missed you, Martha."

Martha chuckled. "I haven't been away long at all."

Mary turned to David. "Are you coming in for some lemonade?"

Jessie made a grunting sound. David cast a look at his *schweschder*. "*Nee*, I would like to, but Jessie needs to run an errand." He pulled a rueful face and then clicked his horse into a trot. Mary watched as they drove away.

Martha had long wondered whether Mary had a little crush on David, and lately she was beginning to wonder if that crush was, in fact, reciprocated.

Mary caught Martha watching her and flushed beet red. "Did you just get here, Martha? Oh, silly me. Of course you just got here, because I saw you pay the taxi when we arrived. So how long are you here for? You've not finished your *rumspringa* already, have you? I mean, I know it's rude of me to ask. Please forgive me." She paused to catch her breath, and added, "But are you still on *rumspringa*?"

Mary laughed. "*Jah*, I'm still on *rumspringa*. It's just that I changed into Amish clothes before I visited *Mamm*, so she wouldn't be upset with me."

"Your mother is not upset with you for going on *rumspringa*, surely?" Mary asked. "Everyone goes on *rumspringa*. I know Hannah and Esther didn't go on *rumspringa* and Rebecca says she doesn't want to, so you must be the only Miller girl who has gone on *rumspringa*."

Martha smiled and walked toward the house. She knew Mary chattered non-stop when she was nervous, and she wondered what had made Mary nervous now. Perhaps it was David Yoder. Aloud she said, "Did you have a good time at the Yoders today, playing with Pirate?"

Mary nodded enthusiastically. "Yes, Pirate is going ever so well. David is training him too, and his training is coming along nicely."

By now, they had reached the Miller *haus*, and both girls walked inside. Mrs. Miller look particularly pleased to see Martha. "I suppose you're not home for good?" she asked hopefully.

"*Nee, Mamm.*" Martha shot her mother a smile.

"Are you here for the day then?" Mrs. Miller asked. Martha nodded. "*Jah.*"

Her mother clasped her hands. "Well then, you can help."

Martha wondered how she could help her mother, given that Rebecca was still at home and Martha was still there helping her mother. Still, she dare not ask. She figured she would find out soon enough.

"We need to make funeral pies and prepare other food," her mother said. "Mr. Hershberger went to be with *Gott.*"

Martha was surprised. "Oh dear. He had been ill for some time, hadn't he?"

Her mother nodded. "Well, come on, the three of

us can make funeral pies, and then Martha, you can visit your *schweschder.*"

"Which one?" Martha asked. "Hannah or Esther?"

"Esther needs some help," her mother said. "She is suffering quite badly from morning sickness. It would be good if you could go to her house and prepare food for them to eat." Mrs. Miller stopped speaking and appeared to be considering her words. She added, "Not that I think Esther is able to eat much, but Jacob certainly will. I'll prepare some more ginger juice for you to take to her to settle her stomach. And make sure she eats some saltine crackers, because they will help keep the nausea away."

"*Jah, Mamm,*" Martha said automatically. She wondered why her mother hadn't asked her what she had been doing while on *rumspringa,* but that was no surprise. She could see Mary was desperate to know, but figured she wasn't going to ask when Mrs. Miller was present.

Finally, Mrs. Miller went outside to the herb garden to gather some ginger for the juice. Mary wasted no time asking her. "Martha, quickly, tell me! What's *rumspringa* like?"

Rebecca too appeared keen to know. "Do you dress like an *Englischer*? What's it like?"

Martha held up one hand to stave off the barrage of questions. "It's very different."

Rebecca rolled her eyes. "Obviously. What do you do?"

"I have a part-time job," Martha said, and that brought gasps from the other two girls.

"Doing what?" Rebecca asked her.

"A cook in a café quite close to my apartment," Martha told her. "The people are nice. Sheryl, my roommate, is nice too. And so is Gary."

"Gary!" both girls shrieked in unison.

"He's an *Englischer*, right?" Rebecca asked her. "Do you like him?"

Martha shook her head. "*Nee*, not like that. We're just friends. Anyway, they don't take any time preparing food and they put it in the microwave. Oh, I mean Sheryl does. I don't know what other *Englischers* do, because I'm only speaking from my experience. She does everything in a hurry, but then she watches television for hours every night. She sits there and doesn't move unless she gets up to fetch something to eat."

"Have you used a microwave yet?" Rebecca asked her.

"No. It seems a little scary, to be honest." She chuckled.

"What's it like watching television?" Mary asked her.

"It was exciting at first, but it's boring sitting there for hours watching it. I'm not used to being idle."

A wistful look passed over Mary's face. "I'd like to try being idle, at least for a time."

Both Martha and Rebecca laughed. "Well, it's different. That's to be sure," Martha said.

"Do you think you'll be on *rumspringa* for a whole year?" Rebecca asked her.

Martha shrugged one shoulder. "I'm just going to play it by ear for now. I need to get my chocolate business going, and I haven't done much work on it yet."

"Well, it all sounds very exciting," Rebecca said, just as Mrs. Miller barged into the room.

"What sounds exciting?" Mrs. Miller asked her.

"Martha being on *rumspringa*," Rebecca said in a small voice.

Mrs. Miller waved a wooden ladle at her. "*Nee*, it is not exciting! Don't you get any ideas, Rebecca. Of course, if you wish to go on *rumspringa*, then that is fine with me." She pulled a face as she said it.

The girls exchanged glances and Mrs. Miller banged a few pots around. Martha knew that meant she was angry, but why she was angry, Martha had no idea. It was normal for the *youngie* in Amish communities to go on *rumspringa*. In most communities, *rumspringa* was the time when a youth left the community and was no longer subject to the usual rules. At the end of *rumspringa*, the youth decided whether to leave the community or to be baptized within the Amish.

Then it occurred to Martha that Mrs. Miller might feel badly toward *rumspringa* because Noah was on *rumspringa* when he lost control of his borrowed car on an icy road and hit the Millers' buggy, leaving all the Miller girls with serious injuries. It had taken months for their injuries to heal, and Rebecca had been in hospital longer than the others. Martha slowly nodded to herself. Yes, that most likely was the source of Mrs. Miller's dislike of *rumspringa*.

Mr. Miller came in the door. "Martha!" he exclaimed, a wide smile on his face. "It is *gut* to see you. Are you enjoying your *rumspringa*?"

Martha broke out into a smile. "*Jah, Datt*, I'm enjoying it so far."

Mr. Miller smiled and nodded. "Are you staying for lunch?"

Mrs. Miller answered. "Yes, she is, and then she's going to visit Esther."

Noah came in the door behind Mr. Miller. Both *menner* walked over to sit at the big wooden dining table. Mrs. Miller pointed to Martha. "Martha, make yourself useful. Make us all some meadow tea. Bring out some whoopie pies and some sugar cakes. Rebecca and Mary, come; sit at the table now."

Martha hurried alone to the kitchen to make meadow tea and fetch food for everyone. She realized her mother was punishing her, but she didn't care. She enjoyed visiting with her parents, but this was no longer her way of life. She was going to be an *Englischer* now, and she very much doubted whether she would return from her *rumspringa*.

After Mr. Miller and Noah went back to the workshop, Martha helped her mother, Rebecca, and Mary make funeral pies. Martha knew that raisin pies had been around Amish communities for a very long time. As raisins were available at any time of year, a raisin pie could be made with scarcely a moment's notice and did not require refrigeration. As people always brought food to funerals and viewings, raisin pies soon became a favorite at funerals and this lead to them being known as 'funeral pies.'

Martha beat the eggs with a hand whisk, remembering when she had beaten the eggs at Sheryl's with an electric beater. The beater sure was faster.

Martha put raisins, water, finely grated orange zest, and orange juice in a saucepan and waited for it to come to the boil so she could simmer it.

The hours passed quickly, and soon Martha found herself helping prepare lunch. Over lunch, Mrs. Miller asked Martha, "Are you going to the funeral?"

"I might be able to go to the viewing," Martha said, "but I don't know if I can go to the funeral because I have to work every morning."

Her mother screwed up her nose in an expression of distaste.

"Now Rachel, leave Martha alone. She's on her *rumspringa*, so it's good that she came to visit us at all."

Mrs. Miller shot a dark look at her husband from under her lashes. "*Jah*," she said, not too happily.

The lunch, however, was a happy meal, with Mary entertaining everyone with stories of Pirate's antics.

After lunch, Martha helped her *mudder* clear the plates away. "I'd best visit Esther now before it gets any later."

"*Jah*," Mrs. Miller said. "Here, take this ginger oil to her and see what you can do to help."

As Martha drove the buggy to visit with Esther, she once more considered the two different ways of life. Perhaps it was good to do nothing and watch television, after all. Sheryl continually insisted it was relaxing. Martha found feeding the chickens relaxing and knitting relaxing, but she didn't find television relaxing at all. "Maybe I'll get used to it when I become more *Englisch*," Martha said aloud, smiling to herself.

"Oh no, not again." Martha arrived with the bucket just in time. She placed the bucket on the floor under Esther's face, and held back Esther's hair. "That was a close one."

Esther leaned her head back into the pillow.

"I brought a wet wash cloth for your head," Martha added. "And *Mamm* sent ginger juice."

"*Denki*." Esther's reply was breathless.

Martha arranged the cool cotton wash cloth on her *schweschder's* head and walked to the window. From the second story window she could see much of the Hostetlers' farm. There was no sign of Moses.

Martha wondered why Esther was suffering so poorly with morning sickness when Hannah had no morning sickness at all. It hardly seemed fair. At hearing her *schweschder* groan, she turned around. "Do you want something, Esther?"

"*Nee*, I just don't want to feel sick anymore."

Martha thought that being that sick day after day would be awful, but surely it would be all worth it in the end to have a *boppli* to hold in her arms. Martha shrugged. She dare not offer Esther any food. She had done that once already with disastrous results. Jacob had warned her never to mention food until lunchtime and never in the mornings.

Esther stirred again. "*Denki* for coming to look after me, Martha."

"I'm glad to be of help." Martha was indeed glad to be of help to Esther, but she was frustrated that she could not do any work on her business while she was away looking after Esther. There were so many things that she should have been doing. She had to return calls to the wholesaler to get quotes for buying her ingredients in bulk and then there were the packaging people to deal with. She had tracked down a place in California that made the foils that she wanted for her cream centers. There were so many loose ends and so many things to do. She took a deep breath that was bordering on a sigh and sat on Esther's bed, leaning over her to straighten the wash cloth that was threatening to slip off Esther's face.

"That's fine, just leave it. I like it over my eyes." Esther's voice was weak.

Martha knew that morning sickness was a normal part of pregnancy for many women, but she couldn't help but worry if the baby was all right. *How will the baby get nutrients if Esther is hardly eating?* she thought. *I hope that I never have morning sickness.* It was hard for Martha to see Esther so sick. It brought back bad memories of when they had the buggy accident and all her *schweschders* were injured. That had been a hard time for the whole *familye* and it was the cause of their *mudder* disliking the Hostetlers, but now, with Hannah having had twins, her *mudder* had made her peace with her in-laws, the Hostetlers.

Martha smiled as she recalled how Noah and Hannah had finally gotten married and now had two beautiful *bopplin*, a boy and a girl.

Esther's voice broke into her daydreaming. "You don't have to sit here with me on the bed, Martha."

"Okay, I'll go and get the midday meal ready for when Jacob comes home."

As soon as the word *meal* came out of Martha's mouth, she knew she had said the word she was warned never to say—and the effect was instant.

Esther flung the wash cloth from her head and lowered her head over the bucket again.

"I'm sorry," Martha said in a very small voice.

Once Esther's head was back on the pillow again, Martha said, "I'll go now."

Esther did not reply and Martha tiptoed out the door.

As soon as Martha entered Esther's kitchen, she immediately felt at home. The kitchen was large and very much like the one in which she had been raised. The kitchen in Sheryl's apartment was far smaller.

There were three loaves of bread, which Jacob said had been brought over this morning freshly baked by his *mudder*, Katie Hostetler. Mrs. Hostetler was delighted to have two *kinskinner* already, with Hannah's twins, and with another on the way thanks to Esther. She had promised to bring over some beef stew the following day. Mrs. Hostetler was a kindly woman, and even more sympathetic as she herself had experienced severe morning sickness when carrying all four of her *sohns*.

Martha decided to make shoo-fly pies, and as there were plenty of apples, Martha thought she'd also make apple pies, and lots of *lattwaerig*, sweet, creamy, apple butter that would then be on hand for Jacob and Esther to spread on bread.

"How is she, Martha?"

Martha looked up to see Jacob standing in the doorway, his face white and drawn, and full of concern. "She's sleeping now. Last time I checked on her, she said the nausea had gone and she was exhausted."

Jacob's face filled with relief. "*Jah*, the nausea seems to go around noon. The *doktor* said that morning sickness can last all day and night, and that the term 'morning sickness' is somewhat of a misnomer, but in Esther's case, it actually does only last the morning. That said, sometimes it does come in another wave around dinner time if she smells meat cooking."

Martha immediately swung around to the *schnitz und knepp* on the stove. "Oh dear, I have a lot of pork in with the dried apples and dumplings."

Jacob waved her concerns aside. "That should be okay. There are about five or so hours in the afternoon when she's fine."

"Thank goodness. So you must be really excited and looking forward to the *boppli*."

Jacob's face lit up. "*Jah*, we're blessed to be having a *boppli* so soon after we married. I'm so worried about Esther being sick, but the *doktor* said it happens to lots of women. Even the midwife said she'd had very bad morning sickness herself with all her *kinner*. Same with *Mamm*." Jacob pulled out a chair from the dining table in the kitchen and sat down. "So how are you going, Martha?"

Martha was enjoying her busy day with Esther, because she didn't have time to think of her own problems. Although her new job meant that she didn't have to think about trying to find a new place to live and she didn't have to think about her savings getting lower and lower, she suddenly realized she was somewhat alone in the strange and bustling world of the *Englischers*.

"I'm fine." Martha laughed, but even she was aware that it was not joyous laughter. It was more of a forced cackle. "Don't worry about me; I'm fine," she repeated, not too convincingly.

"You sure now? I know it can't be easy in the *Englisch* world by yourself with no one to rely on when you're used to having the community around."

"*Jah*, I'm noticing now that I've left, just how *gut* it is to have the community. They're like one big *familye*."

Jacob smiled at her, but his face looked worn and worried. "If you need anything at all, anything, you know Esther and I are here to help you, don't you?"

"*Jah, denki*, Jacob."

Jacob gave the table a slap with his hand. "Now I'd better go and see how my *fraa* is doing."

"Lunch won't be long. Sorry I didn't have it ready in time."

"You're doing a *wunderbar* job, Martha."

Martha smiled to herself as Jacob hurried up the stairs to see Esther. *They are truly a good match*, she thought. *Esther is very blessed.*

Both her *schweschders* had been blessed to

marry such *wunderbar menner* and they were both Hostetlers, and *bruders* at that. Her friend, Mary, had teased her that she would marry another of the Hostetler boys. Martha considered Mary a little cruel, and at any rate, her *mudder* might not be happy if yet another of her *dochders* married a Hostetler. Her *mudder* did appear to be fine with the Hostetler *familye* now, and Martha did not want to do anything to jeopardize that.

Martha always knew she would get married some day, but getting married and being sick in a bed like Esther was for most of the day, was not something she wanted to do anytime soon. Besides, unlike her *schweschders*, she had career goals. Her chocolate business was going to become a global brand. She was sure of that. Maybe after she achieved success, she would think of marriage and *bopplin*, but not before then.

As Martha stirred the gravy on the gas stove, she compared the Amish life to the *Englisch* life she'd known so far. The *Englisch* life was fast paced and exciting, whereas the Amish life was slow, and seemed to be the same every day. Martha was glad to have some color in her life at last.

Martha served the mashed potatoes with noodles and vegetables on the table, and just as she had laid it all out, Jacob came down the stairs.

"That was *gut* timing! It's ready."

"*Denki*, Martha."

"Is Esther well enough to eat?"

Jacob shrugged. "She said she would try to eat a little. *Mamm* says it's best if she tries to eat."

"Excellent, I'll take some up to her."

As Jacob ate his food, Martha fixed Esther some food on a tray.

"Lemonade too. She likes lemonade," Jacob said. "There's some in the cooler."

"Oh *gut*, she needs to keep her fluids up. She said that's what the midwife told her." Martha poured the lemonade into a glass, placed it carefully on the tray with the food and carried it upstairs.

"How are you now?"

Esther was sitting up a little higher propped up by pillows. "Oh, I'm sorry to be such a bother. This reminds me of the time when we were all hurt from that buggy accident."

Martha placed the tray carefully on her lap and placed the lemonade on the nightstand. "I know." Martha giggled. "I was just thinking that myself."

"I don't like to be a bother."

"Nonsense, it's no bother at all. Besides you might come and help me if I am like this in a few years."

Esther smiled and said, "Of course I will."

Martha did not add that it would be a great many more years before she would have *bopplin*. She was sure that she was the only girl in the community who did not want lots of *bopplin*. *Nee*, she was a career woman and two *bopplin* were as many as she wanted. She might even have an *Englisch* husband and he would definitely not be a Hostetler. Martha wanted to chuckle at her thoughts, but held in her laughter.

Moses Hostetler was a *gut* friend and if she wanted to marry an Amish *mann*, he would make a fine husband, but Martha wanted more out of life than any other Amish girl she knew.

"Is Jacob still here?" Esther asked.

"*Jah*, he's downstairs eating." Martha picked up the cold wash cloth off the bed to take downstairs. "Do you want me to go get him?"

"*Nee*, he'll come and see me before he goes back to work."

Martha nodded. "Do you want me to stay for a few days?"

"*Nee*, I've got *Mamm* coming tomorrow. She's staying until I feel better. *Mamm* said that she had morning sickness just like I have, and when she got to fourteen weeks—bam! She woke up one morning and it was gone, and never came back. It was like that with all four of us, although *Mamm* said her morning sickness wasn't as bad as mine."

"I didn't know that." Martha was surprised to hear. Their *mudder* rarely talked about anything personal. Nevertheless, Martha was relieved, relieved that her *mudder* was going to look after Esther and relieved that she could finally get back to the huge pile of work that was waiting for her. She was even looking forward to seeing Gary Wright.

After Jacob ate what appeared to be a mountain of food, he said goodbye to Esther and made his way back to work.

"What are you doing, Martha?"

Martha swung around from the sink where she was

washing the dishes, to see Esther standing there, with a little color back in her face. Martha quickly pulled out a chair from the table for Esther. "Sit here. Do you feel any better?"

"*Jah*, I always feel better at this time of day and then I think that I'm never going to be sick again. Then it starts again in the mornings." Esther pulled a face. "Sometimes cooking smells make me a little nauseous as well."

Martha patted Esther on the shoulder. "I'll make us some meadow tea." She was grateful to have this quiet time with her *schweschder*. Since Esther had married Jacob, they had hardly spent any time together at all, and it had been the same since their oldest *schweschder,* Hannah, had married. "Your *boppli* and Hannah's *bopplin* will all be a *gut* age to play together when they get older."

Esther patted her tummy, which was barely any bigger than normal. "*Jah*, Jacob and I want to have quite a few *kinner*." Esther looked up at Martha. "What about you, Martha?"

"Do I want *kinner*?" Martha turned away from her to tend to the tea.

"*Jah*, or do you just want to sell your chocolates?" Esther chuckled.

"You must be feeling better if you're able to laugh at me."

"I'm sorry. I'll be serious. I know you want *kinner,* but do you want to have many?"

"I'll have to find a *mann* first, but I would like to have only two or three *kinner*, not a whole bunch."

Esther nodded, and there was a twinkle in her eye. "I've hardly had any time to talk with you, but I remember you did mention that you'd met a nice *Englischer.* Is there anything happening with him?"

"No, not really. We're just friends." Martha found it hard to speak to any of her *schweschders* about dating an *Englischer.* They had never been on *rumspringa,* so they would never be able to understand the things that she was going through, or what it was like to date an *Englischer. Englisch menner* were so different to Amish boys.

"I see. That's probably best. But what about Amish boys? Surely there's a nice Amish boy you like?"

Martha set the cup of meadow tea in front of Esther and sat opposite her. "*Nee*, there are no Amish boys I like, not in that way."

"Hmm. I thought you'd say that." Esther looked up at Martha and chuckled. "I didn't even know that I liked Jacob. It was just something that seemed to happen all of a sudden, even though I'd known him nearly my whole life. Don't let an opportunity pass you by, Martha."

Chapter Four

Martha sat opposite Gary Wright, her neighbor in the upstairs apartment, at a restaurant. She had taken Sheryl's advice, and told Gary she was having dinner with him *just as a friend*. She didn't want to give Gary the wrong idea. He was a handsome *Englischer* and seemed nice, if not a little unusual, and she had always wanted an *Englischer* boyfriend, but she had never dated before and knew that the *Englisch* dated differently from the Amish.

Sheryl had advised her to allow Gary to pay for her, and although Martha hadn't thought that was a good idea, Sheryl had said that was the way it was done. Sheryl had even insisted that Martha borrow her clothes. Martha felt a little uncomfortable in the sky blue, sleeveless, double belted dress, which clung to her figure. It fell to a little above her knees, but thankfully had a modest neckline. It showed off far more skin than Martha was comfortable with, but she was determined to look like an *Englischer*. Sheryl had informed her that it was a Calvin Klein dress, but Martha had no idea what that meant.

Sheryl had even insisted Martha borrow a pearl necklace and matching pearl earrings. Martha had tried to refuse on the basis that they were too expensive, but Sheryl had assured her that they were cheap and fake.

Sheryl had done Martha's hair with an electric-powered instrument Sheryl called a curling iron, and had also done her make-up. Martha had been afraid she would look like a clown, but instead had gasped with delight when Sheryl finally allowed her to look in the mirror. Her long, chestnut hair fell about her shoulders in waves, and the makeup was subtle. In fact, it didn't look so much like make-up, more like an even skin tone and glowing skin.

Martha allowed herself a small prideful moment. After all, she was living as an *Englischer* now.

Martha turned her attention back to Gary, who was studying the menu. He was more handsome when he wasn't speaking, as he loved to pull silly faces or make exaggerated expressions when he was talking.

Gary looked up and saw Martha watching him. "I'm paying for you, Martha, if that's okay?" When she nodded and thanked him, he added, "And you don't have to choose the cheapest thing on the menu to be polite. That's what I did when I was a student and people paid for my dinner." Gary laughed loudly and slapped one hand on the table, causing other patrons to turn and look at him.

"So what do you do, Gary?" Martha asked. "Are you a musician, or do you do something else?"

Gary looked affronted. "No, I wouldn't make money out of music. That wouldn't be right to make money from an artistic endeavor. That would be selling out! No, I'm an accounts executive."

"Oh." Martha had no idea what an accounts executive was, but it did sound impressive. Gary was better dressed than usual tonight too, not in the same shabby clothes he wore around the apartment. *Well, why would he wear the same clothes all the time?* she scolded herself. *Moses wears farm clothes most times, but he wears good clothes to church meetings.* Still, Martha didn't care what someone wore—it was what was inside that counted.

If only Moses was an Englischer, Martha thought. She'd had a crush on Moses for years, but was determined to make her way in the *Englisch* world. She knew Moses would never leave the Amish. He wouldn't even go on *rumspringa*, despite the fact that his oldest *bruder*, Noah, had. Moses said he was just wasn't interested.

Sitting there, Martha could not help herself making comparisons between the two men. Gary was pale and slender, and had soft hands. By contrast, Moses was broad-shouldered, tall and thick set, with big muscles from all his farm work. Moses set her heart aflutter, whereas Gary had no effect on her whatsoever. Still, one of the television shows that Sheryl made her watch said women take a while to be attracted to a man. Martha was determined to give Gary a chance.

Martha looked around the restaurant. There were as many *Englischers* here as there were Amish eating in a shift after a Singing, but here, men and women were eating together. Instead of gas lighting, there was electric lighting that was turned down to promote a cozy ambience, but it still felt harsh to Martha. There were heavy, gilt mirrors everywhere, and Martha felt herself looking at them constantly. She had barely seen a mirror in her entire life, and it seemed that the *Englisch* world was full of mirrors of every shape and description.

The wall behind Gary was glass and presumably had been designed to afford patrons a clear view of the wine cellar. Martha's community didn't drink, although people on *rumspringa* were allowed to drink. Martha didn't feel comfortable drinking, so declined when Gary asked her if she'd like some wine.

"You don't mind if I drink then, do you?" Gary asked.

"No, of course not." Martha was relieved that Gary didn't ask her any questions about not drinking.

Martha looked down the menu. Everything looked so fancy. She'd never been to a restaurant before, and had looking forward to the experience, but now she was a little daunted.

"You can't decide?"

Martha looked up at Gary. "No, it's a bit different from Amish food."

Gary scratched his head. "Do you like chicken?"

Martha nodded.

"Well, there's the grilled chicken, and it has mozzarella cheese, olives, roasted red peppers, and pesto sauce. If you like chicken, that would be a good choice." He stabbed his finger at the menu. "Oh, and you could try the marinated, grilled shrimp. It has some sort of sauce. I don't know what the Italian word means so it's anyone's guess what type of sauce—and roasted garlic and Edam cheese. It has roasted red peppers too. What do you think?"

Martha wasn't sure. She had intended to be adventurous, but there were so many strange choices. "I'll have the chicken, I think."

Gary nodded his approval. "Wise choice."

When the meals arrived, Martha shut her eyes and bowed her head for a minute. When she looked up, she saw that Gary was staring at her. "I was giving thanks to *Gott* for the meal," she said by way of explanation.

"You could have said it aloud if you'd wanted. There's no one close."

Martha hurried to explain. "Oh, it's not that. It's what we always do. We offer up a silent prayer before and after a meal."

Gary raised his eyebrows. "After too? That's cool. Go ahead then."

"Um, I've already prayed," Martha said. She found Gary a little strange. However, he appeared to be relaxed about everything, but she wasn't entirely comfortable with him like she was with Moses. *It's probably because he's an* Englischer, she thought.

Gary also often seemed to go off into his own world, staring into the distance with a dreamy expression on his face. Martha supposed it was because he was an artistic type.

Gary was in one of his moments now, so Martha took the opportunity to study the restaurant again. The walls were painted a golden yellow with some sort of paint effect that made them look like real gold in the reflected light. The tablecloths were white and were laid over dark blue tablecloths. *They must be doing laundry every day with these white tablecloths*, Martha thought. *They'd get awfully messy.* The opulent curtains looked expensive and were of shiny olive green, matching the tall, elegant water bottles on each table.

The chairs were upholstered and remarkably comfortable. *I wish the benches at church meetings were as comfortable as this*, Martha thought, wondering if she would ever attend an Amish church meeting again.

"Penny for your thoughts?"

Martha looked up into Gary's inquisitive face. "I was just thinking how different this all is to my old world."

"Different bad or different good?"

Martha shrugged. "I don't know. Neither, I suppose, just different."

She expected Gary to pursue the subject, but he just looked off into the distance again. *He's nothing like Moses*, Martha thought. *I can talk to Moses for hours and never run out things to say, but it's tense and a bit awkward with Gary. Still, I've hardly known Gary long at all. I'll have to get over Moses if I'm going to live in the* Englisch *world. He'd never leave the Amish.* And with that, Martha resolved to give Gary a chance. He was a handsome and thoughtful *Englischer*, and if she pined after Moses, she'd just end up back with the Amish.

"Gary, do you believe in God?" she blurted.

Gary jumped a little. "Yes, I thought I told you."

"No?"

"Yes, I said I play in a worship band."

Martha couldn't see the connection. She had no idea what a worship band was. She didn't know whether to ask outright or to pretend she knew what he meant, but finally asked, "What's a worship band?"

"I play at church every Sunday." Gary stared at Martha, and then continued. "At our church, we have a band, for the praise and worship songs."

"You sing to music? What sort of music?"

"All sorts. We have slow music, but we have fast and loud music too, with drums. We're *happy clappers*." He chuckled long and hard.

The waiter returned to take their dessert orders. Martha again decided not to be daring and selected a strawberry sponge cake soaked in sweetened condensed milk and topped with cream, while Gary chose Red Rose Chocolate Layer Cake.

"Happy clappers, is that what you said?" Martha had never heard the term. The *Englisch* churches sounded very different indeed and quite complicated.

Gary laughed. "That's what some other churches

call us. We're Pentecostal. I go to an Assemblies of God church."

"Oh. So it's not a Catholic or Baptist church?"

"No." Gary chuckled. "Would you like to come along one day and see for yourself?"

"Oh yes, I'd love to. Thanks."

Perhaps I will like Gary's church, Martha thought. *I will have to find a church to attend if I'm going to be an* Englischer. Her thoughts turned to Gary. *It's good he believes in* Gott *and goes to church*, she thought, *but he's so different from Moses. I need to find an* Englisch mann *who is just like Moses.*

Chapter Five

Martha had never been so nervous preparing a meal for other people. Sheryl, of course, was coming, and she had invited Gary, as well as a waitress from work, Laura. Laura had been friendly to Martha ever since she'd started working there, and lived nearby. She had confided to Martha that she was lonely, so Martha thought that Laura would enjoy coming for dinner.

The six layer dinner was coming along nicely, but Martha was having trouble with the desserts. She had made an applesauce cake and a chocolate pie. Yet, when she started making the applesauce cake, the sugar and the shortening did not cream well at all. Likewise, with the chocolate pie, the cream cheese and the sugar seemed to be a funny texture.

Martha just couldn't figure out the problem. She had never had a cooking problem before, but then again, her *mudder* and her *schweschders* had always been there to help. Now she was on her own. Martha fought back the urge to cry. *You're being silly,* she silently scolded herself. *Pull yourself together.* That was what Mrs. Miller always said, and it made Martha smile.

The chocolate pie was in the refrigerator, and the applesauce cake was prepared ahead, and was also in the refrigerator, as Martha intended to take it out and bake it just as she was about to serve the six layer dinner.

Martha hurried around with the vacuum cleaner. She was used to a small battery-operated vacuum cleaner for her parents' sofas, but Sheryl had a big vacuum cleaner that Martha found far more effective than a straw broom on the polished wooden floors. Sheryl wasn't the tidiest person either, so Martha worked hard making the apartment look spic and span for her guests.

When Martha turned off the vacuum cleaner, she heard her cell phone, but she had no idea where she'd left it. She finally found it in the kitchen, but it had stopped ringing by then. She picked it up and saw she had a missed call from Sheryl. Just then Sheryl called again, the ring tone startling Martha. "Sheryl!" Martha's voice came out like a screech.

Sheryl came straight to the point. "Look, Martha, you know how I said to feel free to use my flour and sugar and stuff for dinner tonight?"

Martha nodded and then realized that Sheryl could not see her. "Yes."

"Okay, well, I forgot to tell you something. I have sugar in the container marked *Salt* and salt in the one marked *Sugar.* Hello, Martha, are you there, hello?

But the flour is in the flour container, so don't worry about that. I keep meaning to change them over, but I keep forgetting. Anyway, I'll be home soon." Sheryl hung up without another word.

Martha was speechless. She hurried to the refrigerator and carefully took out the two pies. She took a teaspoon and scooped out a little piece of the Chocolate Pie. It tasted like salt. She tried the Applesauce Cake. To her dismay, it tasted like salt too. For a moment Martha was annoyed with Sheryl, but after all, Sheryl had no idea how to bake and probably had no idea how long food took to prepare.

What was she to do? There was no time to prepare anything else, and just the six layer dinner by itself would hardly be satisfying. *I wanted to be an* Englischer, Martha thought, *and my first attempt at having people for dinner, and look what's happened.* She threw the pies in the trash, and then tried to figure out what to do next. There was barely any sugar left. In fact, there wouldn't even have been enough to use for the two pies she'd already made.

She sighed aloud as her cell phone rang again. "What is it, Sheryl?"

"Martha, it's me."

"Moses! Oh sorry, I forgot you said you would call me once a week." Martha immediately felt bad for saying that, so tried to cover up. "Sorry, that came out wrongly," she said quickly, her words tumbling one over the other. "I'm just a bit stressed. I made two pies for dessert, but Sheryl just called and said that she had the salt in the sugar container, so I've just had to throw the pies out. My guests will be here soon and I don't have any dessert."

"Just wait a moment, can you, Martha?"

"Sure."

Moses returned to the phone. "I'm in my *mudder's* store, not far away at all, and *Mamm* has a shoo-fly pie here. She said you can have it."

Martha made to protest, but Moses was still speaking. "I'll be right there. We're just leaving."

Martha thanked Moses but he'd already hung up. "Thank you, *Gott*," she said aloud, looking up at the ceiling. Martha hurried to the bathroom to apply make-up the way Sheryl had shown her. Sheryl continually encouraged Martha to use her make-up, and Martha had started to wear a little make-up to work. Now she applied a mineral face primer, followed by a light foam foundation. She sucked in her cheeks and brushed on the bronzer, but put on too much, so she had to scrub most of it off.

Sheryl had tried to encourage Martha to wear mascara, but her lashes were already long and dark, and the mascara made Martha's eyes sore. She put the tube of mascara back in the box, but took out some dark brown eye shadow, and applied it to fill in her eyebrows. Then she brushed her long hair. Sheryl would have wanted her to use the curling iron, but Martha wasn't quite ready to try that by herself just yet.

Martha carefully put on the dress that Sheryl had laid out for her to wear. Sheryl had described it as a *Valentino, fit-and-flare, double-knit dress*, but all

Martha could see was that it was bright red. The brightest color Martha had ever worn in her life was purple, a subdued purple at that, and even the sky blue dress she had worn to dinner with Gary could be called muted by comparison.

Oh well, I'm an Englischer *now*, Martha told herself as she slipped the dress over her head. Nevertheless, when she looked at her reflection in the full-length mirror, she felt somewhat guilty. The dress fell to her knees, but the material a few inches above her knees was lace, so her legs could still be seen. At least the crew neckline was modest, despite the lace panel on the neckline. The sleeves were short. The rib-knit banding at intervals down the dress ensured that the dress clung to her figure, and while it was not too tight, it was certainly far more figure hugging than an Amish girl was used to.

Martha jumped when she heard a knock on the door, so hurried over to open it. Moses was standing in the doorway, and his jaw dropped open at the sight of her. "Martha! You look, *um*, great."

"Thank you, Moses." Martha was a little embarrassed, and so spoke formally. Her community was not in the habit of complimenting anyone, but she realized that Moses must be quite surprised to see her in *Englischer* clothes for the first time. "Come in."

Moses was still standing in the doorway. "I've never seen you in a dress before."

Martha had no idea what he was talking about. "But I've always worn dresses," she protested.

"Not like that." Moses's jaw was still hanging open. He walked in and Martha looked behind him.

"Where's your *mudder*?"

"She kept going. I'll get a taxi home." He handed the pie to Martha.

"*Denki, denki* so much." Martha smiled. "That was so good of you to come to my rescue."

"I'll always come to your rescue, Martha." Moses smiled at her, and her heart leaped in response.

"Stay for dinner," she said on impulse.

Moses looked embarrassed. Little red patches formed on his tanned cheeks. "*Nee*, I couldn't really."

"Oh please, Moses. There's only my roommate, Sheryl, and two other people. It would be great if you could stay. I'd like you to meet Sheryl. She's been so kind to me. She's always lending me stuff, and she's very nice."

Moses looked doubtful, so Martha added, "Please, Moses, and you're catching a taxi home anyway. It's not as if your *mudder's* out there waiting for you."

Moses agreed—reluctantly, or so it seemed to Martha. She felt a little hurt.

Chapter Six

Gary was the first guest to arrive. Martha showed him into the living room where she and Moses had been sitting, chatting. "Gary, this is Moses, Moses Hostetler."

Gary walked over and held out his hand. "Mr. Hostetler."

Martha had no idea that Gary was speaking formally as his idea of a little joke, so she decided to follow suit and introduce Gary in the same way. "And Moses, I'd like you to meet Mr. Wright."

Moses looked horrified. "What? Oh, I mean congratulations. Isn't this very sudden though?" His face flushed beet red.

Martha had no idea what he was talking about, but Gary burst out laughing. "No, my name is Gary Wright, Wright with a *W*. Martha doesn't mean Mr. Right with an *R*." Gary fell onto the sofa and collapsed into helpless peals of laughter, while both Moses and Martha stood by, embarrassed.

Martha was mortified, but was saved by another knock at the door. This time it was Laura, and she had brought with her a box of chocolates. "Hi, Martha, here's a box of chocolates. I feel silly bringing you chocolates with you being a chocolate expert and all, but I know you don't drink wine."

Martha was overcome by Laura's thoughtfulness. "Come in. I don't have any chocolates left, apart from the samples I need this week, so this is perfect, *denki*, um, thank you."

This time she introduced the two men as *Moses* and *Gary*, and Gary caught her eye and chuckled. Martha didn't find it at all amusing, so looked away. Gary's face lighted up at the sight of Laura, and so did Moses's face, Martha thought. She wondered if this dinner party was such a good idea after all. Besides, how would Moses, an Amish man, relate to the *Englischers*? Well, she herself was Amish, although she had one foot firmly in the *Englisch* world now. Martha hoped that the night would not prove to be a disaster.

Martha was in the kitchen checking the six layer dinner when she heard Sheryl arrive and introduce herself. Martha was pleased. She'd had enough of introductions for one day. Her face felt hot as she remembered that Moses had thought that she was introducing Gary as *Mr. Right*. Anyway, whatever was she thinking having both men to dinner? She had feelings for Moses, and she had kind of been dating Gary. She hoped Gary wouldn't mention their dinner date to Moses.

Sheryl popped her head into the kitchen. "Need any help?"

"No thanks. It's under control. Oh, Sheryl, you don't mind me serving food in this dress, do you? I couldn't find an apron."

Sheryl waved her concerns away. "That's just a cheap dress. Don't worry about spilling anything on it. There are more dresses where that came from. It looks good on you. You should've worn some make-up, though."

I am wearing make-up, Martha thought with dismay. *Perhaps I didn't put enough on.*

When Martha brought out the food, the four were talking happily. She was relieved that Moses didn't seem to feel out of place with three *Englischers*. In fact, he was talking quit a lot and Laura was hanging on his every word. That fact caused Martha a pang of anxiety. She knew she had feelings for Moses, and knew that he would not leave the Amish, and somehow she had reconciled herself to that, or at least she thought so. However, it had not occurred to her until now that if she didn't marry Moses, he would one day marry another. She caught her breath at the thought, but then had to turn her attention to serving the food.

"Is this Amish food?" Gary asked.

"*Jah*, yes, it is."

Gary beamed at Martha and she noticed that Moses was watching closely. *I wonder if Moses is jealous?* she thought. *I'm a little jealous that Moses is speaking to Laura.*

Laura was seated next to Moses and he was telling her all about Amish food. "It's amazing you can cook so much without electricity," she said, touching his arm and smiling at him.

"We have gas or wood stoves," Moses said, but Martha interrupted with a laugh.

"The women do all the cooking. Moses has never baked anything in his life. Isn't that right, Moses?"

Moses chuckled. "That's true, but I do know that we have a gas stove as well as a wood stove."

"Laura, Martha said you work with her?" Gary appeared to be trying to take Laura's attention away from Moses, and Martha didn't know whether to be pleased or irritated. Laura was turning out to be quite the flirt. Still, Martha had to admit that Laura had no idea that she herself had been to dinner with Gary, nor that she harbored feelings for Moses.

"Wow, this dinner is so good, Martha." Gary winked at her.

It was obvious to Martha that Moses saw Gary wink and didn't like it. *Surely Moses knows there's no hope of anything between us*, Martha thought. *I told him I wouldn't go back to the Amish. Perhaps I shouldn't have invited him for dinner. It might've made things more complicated.* Then Martha realized that she would have to stop calling on Moses every time she needed help, and she wasn't quite prepared to do that, not yet. How could she reconcile her feelings for Moses with the fact that she wanted to remain in the *Englisch* world? She had never heard of a married couple where one person was Amish and the other an *Englischer,* with both of them living in their own worlds. Was that even possible?

After the six layer dinner, Martha cleared the plates with Laura's help. When the two of them were alone in the kitchen, Martha explained how Sheryl had the salt in the sugar container, much to Laura's amusement.

"Hey, Martha, if you don't mind me saying so, how can you afford such an expensive dress?" Laura asked. "I'm sure you don't get paid more than I do, and I certainly couldn't afford it. Are the Amish very wealthy?"

"Oh no," Martha hastened to explain. "It's not my dress. It's Sheryl's. I don't have many *Englischer* clothes and Sheryl always lets me borrow hers."

Laura nodded, but still looked puzzled. "How does Sheryl afford it then? And that dress she's wearing— it looks like a designer dress."

Martha shrugged. "No idea. She doesn't like to talk about herself much, but she says the dresses are cheap."

"That explains it then! They must be knock-offs."

Martha was about to ask what a knock-off was, when Laura leaned over and spoke to her in a conspiratorial whisper. "So which one do you want, Moses or Gary?"

Martha's hand flew to her throat. "What do you mean?"

"Oh come on, Martha, don't be coy. They're both good looking guys and you're single. I don't want to step on your toes."

Martha didn't know what to say. "Err, which one do you like?"

Laura giggled. "Both of them, really, but I'll have whichever one you don't want."

"Amish boys don't date *Englischer* girls."

Laura winked at her. "Well, you never know! It's worth a try." Before Martha could say another word, Laura took the shoo-fly pie and headed back to the dining room.

To Martha's dismay, Laura hung on Moses's every word and touched his arm flirtatiously at intervals. Gary spent the evening speaking to Laura too, leaving Sheryl and Martha to talk to each other. It wasn't quite how Martha had planned the evening.

"So how is the chocolate business going, Martha?" Moses asked her.

Martha noticed Laura was visibly put out that Moses was turning his attention to her. "I'm going to sell my chocolates at the market soon, but I have a meeting with a broker. He's a broker for various store buyers."

"That's good." Moses's face lit up.

"It's in New York at the end of the week," Martha said. "They're allowing me to take Thursday and Friday off work so I can go to New York."

Moses gasped. "New York? How can you go to New York?"

Martha took his words literally. "Well, I catch the train of course," she said with a frown.

Moses shook his head. "*Nee*, Martha! You can't go

to New York. You've never been to New York before. Are you going alone?"

Before Martha could respond, Laura spoke. "I wanted to go with her, but I have to cover for her at work."

"So are you going alone?" Moses asked again.

Martha nodded, a small knot forming in the pit of her stomach. She had been deeply concerned about going to New York all by herself, and now Moses was showing such obvious concern, she felt quite foolish about considering the matter in the first place.

Finally, she said, "I have to go. He's a big agent for all the buyers and he only takes five percent I've done a lot of research online, and I'm amazed he's even agreed to speak with me."

Moses rubbed one hand over his forehead. "I'll have to go with you."

Martha was shocked. "Come with me? What about the farm work? And Jacob has to keep checking on Esther so I'm sure he's not working at his full capacity. What will your *vadder* say?"

"I'm sure my parents will think you shouldn't go to New York alone," he said. "Have you told your parents?"

Martha shook her head vigorously. "*Nee*, and please don't tell them, Moses. They wouldn't agree, I'm sure."

Moses appeared to thinking things over. "I'll have to go with you, Martha."

Gary laughed raucously. "Two Amish people wandering around New York? I don't think that's a good idea. I'd go with Martha, but I have a gig on Thursday night that I can't get out of."

Moses screwed up his nose, and Martha could see he didn't like the idea of Gary accompanying her at all. On the other hand, Martha was secretly pleased that Moses had offered to go with her. "Thank you, Moses. Are you sure it will be all right?"

He nodded. "I've never been to New York of course, and I've never been on a train, but I'm sure between the two of us we can figure things out. After all, how hard could it be?"

The *Englischers* at the table looked shocked. "You need to book motel rooms," Sheryl said. "Martha, you haven't booked a room yet, have you?"

Martha was discomforted. "I was going to get your help with doing that."

"Well, it's a bit too late to get discounted tickets, but at least you'll be able to get train tickets. When you get to Penn Station in New York, get a taxi straight to the motel."

Gary interrupted them. "And don't leave the motel at all at night."

Sheryl agreed. "And then the next morning, you should leave for your appointment early, right?" Martha nodded. Sheryl pushed on. "Get a taxi from your motel straight to the appointment. When it's over, get a taxi straight back to your motel. Book a motel with a restaurant so you don't have to leave the building. When it's time for you to leave, get a taxi straight back to Penn Station. Make sure you're early, early so you don't miss the train. Once you're on the train, it will all be fine."

Martha noticed that Gary, Sheryl, and Laura were exchanging glances again. It was clear the three of them thought it was a crazy idea for two Amish people to wander around New York. Martha could see Moses was worried too.

"Thanks for your advice," Moses said. "We will do as you say. Can you recommend a motel?"

"Wait right here." Sheryl left the room and returned presently with a laptop. "What's the broker's address?" she asked Martha.

"I'll just have to check." Martha walked to her bedroom and returned with a piece of paper. She put in front of Sheryl.

Sheryl tapped away at the keyboard. "Okay, I found a motel not too far away, and I can get you the cheaper rates. I'd better book you now. I'll pay online, and you too can pay me back later."

Both Moses and Martha made to protest, but Sheryl said, "I know you probably don't understand, but people pay online these days. You don't turn up to the motel and hand over cash. I'll book two rooms for you now. This motel has reasonable rates and has a restaurant, so you won't need to go out looking for food."

"I'll bring the money for you when I collect Martha," Moses said.

Sheryl shook her head. "How about you come here, Moses, and I'll give you both a ride to the station. When you get back here, Martha can call or text me and I'll come and collect you."

They both thanked her. Martha felt blessed to have such a good friend as Sheryl. It was the same sense of community she had experienced with the Amish.

Sheryl let out a shriek. "Just as well I haven't booked yet! This motel is a short walk from Penn Station. It has a restaurant too. Do you want to see the website?"

Martha shook her head. "Whatever you think is best, Sheryl," Martha said.

"I wish I could come too," Laura said wistfully. "Maybe I could find someone to cover for me."

Martha shot her a weak smile, but didn't say anything. She certainly hoped Laura wouldn't come. If she were to be honest with herself, she would admit she wanted to spend time with Moses, but she couldn't quite bring herself to do so. She did, however, allow herself to admit she was pleased someone was going with her, someone as strong, capable and kind as Moses. Martha had been sick with worry about going to New York by herself, and now she had someone to go with her, even if that person was just as clueless about New York as she herself was.

Laura became more flirtatious as the night went on, hanging on Moses's every word.

As Martha lay in bed that night, looking at the stars through her open curtains, she wondered whether she wanted to be an *Englischer* after all. Being an *Englischer* was turning out to be not quite so much fun.

Chapter Seven

Martha felt her heart lift; today she was going to New York to speak with a broker. She jumped out of bed in a flurry of excitement, but took only two steps before a wave of nausea overcame her. She didn't know if she was more nervous about speaking with a broker, or the fact Moses was accompanying her to New York for two days. Placing a steadying hand against the wall, she took in one big deep breath, and then she walked into the kitchen to make a pot of *kaffi*.

Sheryl made *kaffi* differently. Here the *kaffi* pot was electric, and the brown beans of the coffee were hidden inside an aluminum pod.

"Martha?"

Martha spun around, shocked, her face burning a furious pink. "Sheryl! You never get up so early."

Sheryl laughed as she stepped toward Martha. "I'm driving you to the station. Have you forgotten?"

Martha shook her head. "No, I haven't forgotten."

"Are you nervous?" Without waiting for Martha to reply, Sheryl stood on her tiptoes and fetched a ceramic mug from a top cupboard. "Here, pour some for me, will you?"

Martha did as she was asked.

"You know you can eat on the train, right?"

"Yes," Martha replied. "I thought we'd be allowed to take food on the train. I was going to make some sandwiches."

Sheryl laughed. "No, I'm pretty sure there's a café car on the train, although I haven't caught a train to New York since I was a little kid. When I bought the tickets, there was no mention that they included meals, but you can go along to the café car and buy something."

Martha clutched her throat. If she was so overcome with anxiety at the thought of purchasing a meal on the train, how would she ever cope with going to New York? She felt quite foolish for even thinking it was possible.

Sheryl hurried to reassure her. "You'll be fine, Martha, really. I can see you're worried, but you're looking at the big picture. Just take everything one step at a time. That's what I do when I'm worried about something. I break it down into little pieces. Anyway, you'll probably have more confidence once you arrive in New York because the train ride will be behind you."

Martha shut her eyes and took a deep breath. She exhaled slowly and then opened her eyes. "I do hope you're right," she said in a small voice.

Martha and Sheryl sat at the dining table, eating toast. It was a far cry from Martha's big Amish breakfasts, but at least the *kaffi* had made her feel a little better, like she was at home.

"What are you going to wear?" Sheryl asked her.

"Wear?" Martha repeated.

Sheryl nodded as she swallowed another bit of toast. "Honestly, sometimes I wonder about you, Martha. Just as well we're the same size. You can borrow my jeans. I'll find you something to wear."

"I shouldn't go to see the broker wearing jeans, should I?" Martha asked.

Sheryl shook her head. "No, silly. Come on, I'm going to have to lend you some clothes." With that she took Martha's arm and escorted her into her bedroom. She reached into her closet and pulled out sets of clothes, one after the other. Sheryl held several dresses against Martha before deciding on what she described as a 'slim business pencil dress.' "This will look good to see the broker," she said. "It's knee length and the dark blue sets off your coloring. And take two pairs of jeans. Oh, and you'll need to wear something to the restaurant tonight."

Martha's stomach sank. Going to New York was daunting enough without having all these changes of clothes. Why it was so much easier wearing her Amish clothes, her dress and cape, apron, prayer *kapp*, and bonnet. It was easy when she wore the same thing day after day, and even when she wore fresh clothes, no one could tell them apart from the old ones. Martha reflected that being *Englisch* was quite a lot of work.

Sheryl held up a black lace dress. "Yes, wear this to the restaurant tonight," she said. "Your accommodation comes with a free breakfast, so you won't need to worry about that." Sheryl scratched her head. "You'll have to have lunch on the train. I think I have everything sorted out for you."

"Thanks for being so helpful," Martha said. "I wouldn't have been able to do any of this without you."

Sheryl patted her shoulder gently. "Of course you would! It's no trouble. Oh, and you'll need shoes. Just wear your normal shoes for the train or you might get blisters, but you should borrow the shoes you wore when you had dinner with Gary. Did they hurt your feet?"

Martha assured her that they didn't.

"You can also wear them for the meeting with the broker," Sheryl continued. "You'll need to take more make-up with you too."

Sheryl had already given Martha plenty of make-up, so Martha was surprised she would need more.

"You'll need highlighter," Sheryl continued. "I have some shimmering illuminating powder. New York women are very well groomed, you understand. And maybe you should borrow my straightening iron too."

Martha recoiled in horror. "No, I don't think I could use it."

"I can show you how it works now," Sheryl protested.

Martha shook her head. "No, I really wouldn't use it."

Sheryl sighed in resignation. "Okay, then. You

have to look your best for the meeting with the broker, that's all."

There was a knock on the door. Sheryl answered it. "It's Moses," she called out, somewhat unnecessarily.

Moses entered the apartment, his handsome face bright and beaming. Martha noticed that he was carrying a backpack. As he stepped toward her, she also noticed that familiar Moses smell, soap and sandalwood. It comforted her, and she felt all her tense muscles loosening.

"My *mudder* sent some food for us to eat on the train," he announced, reaching around to pat his backpack.

"Please thank her for me," Martha said, but Sheryl interrupted her.

"Luggage! Martha, you'll have to borrow my Louis Vuitton travel bag."

"What's that?" Martha said, her brow furrowed.

"It's a designer travel bag," Sheryl said. She hurried out of the room and returned with a brown duffel bag. "This is the perfect size. Moses, help yourself to some coffee while Sheryl and I pack."

Moses dug around in his pocket before handing some notes to Sheryl. "Thanks for getting my tickets, Sheryl."

"No problem. Oh that reminds me! I printed the tickets out. I'll fetch them for you."

Moses put the tickets in his backpack and headed for the kitchen. Martha noticed his normally tanned face was white and drawn, and she worried if he was as afraid of going to New York as she was.

Soon the three of them were in Sheryl's car. Martha's stomach was churning and her breath was coming in short sharp bursts. She wondered if it was too late to back out. "It will be all right, Martha," Moses said from the back seat.

Martha looked over her shoulder and smiled. "Thank you for coming with me, Moses."

He shot her a look that made her heart melt. "I couldn't let you go alone, Martha."

After Sheryl parked the car, she said, "I had better come with you just to make sure you get on the train safely."

Martha and Moses thanked Sheryl again. Martha was already a little afraid of the number of people around. "I've never seen so many people in one place," she said to Sheryl.

Sheryl laughed. "This is nothing compared to New York," she said. "Now go on, right through that door there."

Sheryl guided them to collect free luggage tags. "You have to fill out your contact information and attach it somewhere visible on your bags. We still have a while before your train goes. Let's wait in the waiting room," she said.

The three of them sat along a row of chairs. They were the only vacant seats Martha could see. People around them were on their laptops, and suitcases were piled high everywhere. Sheryl tapped Martha's knee. "Now, Martha, I have to tell you about the yellow cabs."

"Cabs?" Martha repeated, looking around her nervously at the people milling about. "I thought you said we could walk to the broker's offices."

Sheryl shrugged one shoulder. "Sure, but I need to tell you just in case. You can't call a yellow cab. You have to flag one. Now, a yellow cab is only on-duty when the middle numbers on its roof are lit. It's off-duty if all the numbers are lit. If you can't see any numbers lit, that means there are already passengers in the cab. Don't try if the middle numbers aren't lit."

Martha was doing her best to remember. "Only if the middle numbers are lit," she repeated. *I'll never remember that*, she thought. It all seemed too hard.

Martha's heart was beating out of her chest. There were *Englischers* scurrying this way and that, all looking as though they knew what they were doing. Englischers *must be very smart people*, she thought. They appeared to have a sense of purpose, whereas she felt frightened, anxious, and alone. However, she was not alone. Moses was sitting next to her. Even his very presence steadied her.

A small child crashing into her made her flinch. A beleaguered woman with wild hair and small, strained eyes apologized to her. She was trying to manage two young children, and Martha watched as the woman arranged one on her hip and put the other in a pram.

"Guys are checking you out," Sheryl said to Martha.

Martha didn't know whether to be pleased or offended, but she could see Moses was decidedly put out. He crossed his arms over his chest and moved a little closer to Martha, and once more she smelled the soap and sandalwood. Her heart fluttered.

"Okay, it's time for you to board now," Sheryl said. "Just remember what I told you, and everything will be okay. Anyways, you can always call or text me, Martha."

As Martha stood up, she felt as though all the blood had drained from her head. She felt dizzy, and everything spun. Martha silently scolded herself. *This is the beginning of your new life as an* Englischer, she said to herself. *You have to go through with this if you're going to have a successful chocolate business.*

Martha found everything daunting: the crowds, the train, and the sensation of rushing energy all around her. Everyone seemed in a hurry. What's more, it was loud. She resisted the urge to put her hands over her ears. Martha considered the place was noisy and dirty, but not dirty in the way a farm was dirty. She wrinkled her nose at the pungent smell of chemicals and fumes.

Martha did not breathe properly until she and Moses were seated on the train. He had kindly allowed her to have the window seat. People were hurrying along the corridors, going this way and that. It was a far cry from the peaceful Amish life to which Martha was accustomed.

"How are you doing, Martha?" Moses asked her.

"I'm really scared, to be honest," she said.

"But you do want to have a chocolate business, don't you?"

Martha nodded. "*Jah*, I do." Martha folded her

arms and set her resolve. Yes, she would have a successful chocolate business. She just had to put on her brave face. After all, what could go wrong? Moses was with her and the train was about to head to New York where she would meet with a broker, and do her best to convince him to put her chocolates before buyers.

It was all Martha could do not to clutch Moses's arm as the train pulled away. Martha, of course, had never been in a train before, and what's more, had only been in a car on those occasions her parents paid a driver take them somewhere further than a buggy could go. The train went faster and faster. She shut her eyes and clenched her hands tightly.

"Martha, Martha," Moses whispered.

She opened one eye and looked at him. "What is it?"

"Are you all right?"

She shook her head. "I've never been so fast. Is it safe?"

Moses smiled at her. "Yes, it's perfectly safe. The *Englisch* ride on these trains all day. It is safe," he said again.

Martha opened her other eye. She looked out the window and gasped as the landscape sped by. "We're on this train for a few hours, aren't we?"

"*Jah.*"

Three hours of doing nothing, Martha thought. *This will be as boring as watching television.* Then again, she realized she couldn't be bored with Moses sitting next to her. She always enjoyed spending time in Moses's company, and now was no exception.

Had it been a mistake for her to allow Moses to accompany her? After all, she wasn't going back to the Amish. If she was, then she could acknowledge her feelings for Moses. *No, that won't do at all*, she silently scolded herself. She was going to have a career. She was going to have a chocolate business, and she was going to become *Englisch*. Moses would only stand in her way. She nodded to herself, earning another worried look from Moses.

His arm accidentally brushed against hers, sending little electric tingles through her. *What am I going to do?* she thought. *I can't be attracted to Moses. I can't think like that.*

Martha shut her eyes and leaned back into the comfortable blue chair. In fact, it was the most comfortable chair in which she had ever sat. Perhaps she could sleep all the way to New York. The train was vibrating in a rather hypnotic way. Martha thought of her chocolates and what she would say to the broker.

The broker had been quite curt in the email Sheryl had helped her send and he had not even spoken with her on the phone. What if her trip to New York proved futile?

No, she had to take the chance. Martha had read many stories on Sheryl's computer telling of people who had persisted to get their businesses started. Martha was determined to be like one of those people. She knew she was no fancy chocolatier, but she also knew that many people liked good, homemade Amish products.

She was drifting off to sleep when she heard Moses's voice. Martha opened her eyes.

"I'm sorry I woke you."

Martha waved his concerns away. "*Nee*, I was just resting my eyes," she said. "What did you say?"

"I asked if you were hungry?"

Martha nodded. "Yes, I'm very hungry, actually. I've only had *kaffi* and toast, not much compared to a big breakfast."

Moses laughed. He stood up to retrieve his bag from the overhead bin. He opened the contents of the bag and showed Martha. "I have freshly cooked eggs, cabbage wedges with peanut butter, and sandwiches, peanuts, and pretzels."

"*Wunderbar*!" Martha exclaimed, just as her stomach grumbled. "I'm starving! What's in the sandwiches?"

"Sliced cheddar, ground ham, onion, and sauerkraut on rye."

As Moses handed Martha a sandwich, she spied something else in his backpack. "Are those sugar cakes?" she asked him.

He laughed. "My mother was worried we'd starve. We can have those next, or wait until later if you like?"

"I wouldn't mind one soon," Martha admitted.

She leaned back in her seat and slowly devoured her sandwich, remembering how good Amish food was. It hadn't been that long since she had started her *rumspringa*, but she already missed Amish food.

Sheryl was a light eater and there was never much food in the house.

Martha looked out at the scenery. The green fields had given way to brown fields. At least she was becoming accustomed to the gentle rocking of the train.

"How was that, Martha?" Moses asked when she finished the sandwich.

"*Wunderbar, denki*," she said.

"Would you like a sugar cake now?"

"Yes, please. Now if only we had *kaffi* to go with it."

"I'll go buy some." Moses made to stand up, but Martha put a restraining hand on his arm.

"*Nee, nee*, Moses. I shouldn't have said anything. It wasn't a hint; I don't need any *kaffi*."

"Sure you do," Moses said with a smile. "I won't be long."

Martha watched anxiously as Moses walked out of sight. She felt bad, as she hadn't meant to hint; she was simply thinking aloud. Would he be able to find the café car of which Sheryl had spoken? She was suddenly afraid to be all alone without Moses.

Martha realized how much she had come to depend on Moses. She knew she could not continue to rely on him, because she was not returning to the community and so would have to rely on her *Englisch* friends instead. Still, she couldn't face not having Moses in her life.

Moses presently returned with two steaming Styrofoam cups of coffee. He handed one to Martha and then sat down. "I don't know how good it is," he said with a shrug.

"*Denki*, Moses." Martha took a sip. "Oh, it's hot! And it is good *kaffi*, after all."

After Martha drank her coffee, she fell asleep. When she awoke, she didn't know where she was. It took her a while to comprehend she was on the train. She sat up, and then saw with horror she had fallen asleep on Moses's shoulder. She hurried to apologize. "Oh, Moses, I'm so sorry. I was in a deep sleep."

"I didn't mind at all," Moses said. He looked at her in a way that made her heart beat faster.

Martha looked around herself nervously. "Are we almost there?"

"Yes, we are," he said. "They announced it would be only another five minutes."

Within seconds, people stood up and took their bags from the overhead bins. It seemed to Martha people were in a mad rush to get off the train before others. She wondered why. "Maybe they have all have urgent business," she said to Moses, who simply shrugged.

"We had better wait until they all leave," he said.

After the flurry of people retrieving bags from the overhead bins and hurrying away, Moses took Martha's bag and his backpack from the overhead bin. "I'll carry your bag for you, Martha," he said.

If Martha had thought the train station at Lancaster busy, the one in New York was immeasurably more so. She didn't know whether to be anxious or exhilarated. People milled around like busy ants hustling and bustling on their way. "Keep close to me," Moses said.

"Sheryl said our motel is quite close to the station. We can walk." Martha was concerned that Moses would try to hail a cab. It sounded all too confusing for her. Small beads of sweat broke out on her forehead at the thought.

If New Yorkers thought the sight of an *Englisch*-dressed girl with an Amish man strange, they didn't show it. No one afforded them a glance. Martha looked around. Penn Station was even bigger than the one in Lancaster. It seemed a little dark to Martha, and she was discomforted when she became aware they were underground.

When Martha and Moses finally found their way out of the station, a crowd of people swept them forward a few paces onto the street. Martha found herself standing not far from a cab. She instinctively looked up to see if the middle lights were on. Just then, someone elbowed her heart out of the way and jumped in the cab, which sped off.

Martha realized she had been pushed onto Moses and her arms were around his neck. She had time to note the surprised look on his face before she pulled away. "I'm sorry, Moses, someone pushed me," she said. Martha could feel her face burning, and imagined it was beet red. Even the tips of her ears were burning.

"Are you all right?" Moses asked, peering into her face.

"*Jah*," she said. "It gave me a fright, that's all. Let's walk to our motel."

To her great relief, Moses took off walking with

his hand on Martha's elbow. She was happy he did not ask to catch a cab.

When they presently came to a towering building, Moses stopped. "This is our motel, I believe."

Martha breathed a huge sigh of relief. "I can't believe it. We made it all this way and we didn't have to catch a cab." Martha felt as if the worst of her ordeal was behind her. She had managed to go on a train and she had made her way successfully from the train station to her motel. Perhaps it wasn't so bad, after all.

"Come on," Moses said in an encouraging tone.

Martha walked into the foyer of the motel and gasped at the opulence. This was a budget motel too, so she wondered what a more expensive motel would look like. The foyer was expansive. She had never seen a ceiling so high. In fact, it was higher than the highest barn she had ever seen. Intricate patterns covered the floor, and heavy chandeliers hung from the ceilings. Couches were placed against the walls. They were in sombre tones and appeared to be of leather, but had plush crimson easy chairs in front of them. Thriving green plants were dotted around the room at intervals. Martha wondered how the plants flourished in there without natural light.

In the middle of the foyer was a huge seating arrangement that was nothing like Martha had ever seen. She looked up at the ceilings once more and saw they were of pressed metal. "This one room is as big as the whole area of the mud sale," she said in wonderment to Moses.

He too appeared surprised. He was standing with

his mouth open. "This place is big," he finally said. "I suppose we had better check in."

When they checked in, Martha and Moses were given a card to swipe for their rooms, and directed to an elevator. In the elevator, Martha suddenly felt afraid. "How does this card work?" she asked Moses.

"I assume you swipe it," he said. "Don't worry. It must be simple."

Martha didn't know why it must be simple, but she trusted Moses. The elevator seemed to take forever and finally opened onto a long corridor. Martha wasn't so sure how she would feel being so high up in a building and in a strange place. They walked down the corridor in silence until they reached Martha's room.

"Let me try to unlock the door," Moses said. He took the card from Martha and inserted it into a little box outside the door. The door opened.

"Aha! I see how it works," Martha said with relief. To be on the safe side, she stuck her foot in the door in case it closed again.

"What time should we meet for dinner?" Moses asked her.

Martha tried to remember what Sheryl had said. "I think Sheryl said she reserved a table for us at seven," Martha told him. "Should we meet at the restaurant?" She was hoping Moses would say he would collect her from her room, and to her relief, he did.

"How about I collect you from your room at seven?"

"But it will take us a while to get there, won't it?" Martha said. "Shouldn't you come earlier?"

Moses chuckled. "The restaurant is just downstairs."

Martha planted her palm on her forehead and laughed too. "Silly me! I'm so used to having to drive a buggy to get somewhere."

"I am buying dinner tonight, Martha, if you have no objection," Moses said, folding his arms over his chest.

Martha remembered Sheryl had told her men felt good when they paid for women. She smiled and said, "That would be lovely. *Denki*, Moses."

Moses smiled and walked away. Martha watched him as he walked down the corridor and opened his door. He looked back over his shoulder and gave a little wave.

Martha smiled and ducked into her motel room. "Whatever will Moses think of me standing there staring at him?" she said aloud to herself. She looked around her room. She had never seen a room like it. A huge painting of flowers hung over the bed, which was quite fancy. The bed was made up with what looked like very expensive linen and had numerous pillows on it. Martha wondered why one person would need more than one pillow. A furry piece of fabric covered one side of the end of the bed. It took Martha a while to realize this was probably for aesthetic effect and had no real purpose.

The carpet was dark green and there was a paler green carpet on top. As well as the cream ruffled pillows, there were fluffy pink cushions on the bed.

"This is all very fancy," Martha said to herself. She

stuck her head in the bathroom door. The bathroom was tiny, all cream and black, and had no windows. Martha did not think she would like to spend long in there at all. She noticed the mirror was large.

Martha returned to the bedroom and looked out the window. She gasped. She hadn't realized she was so high in the sky. Never had Martha been so high, so far away from the ground. She backed away from the window and clutched her throat, and then edged forward a little and pulled the heavy drapes shut as fast as she could.

After a few moments, she shuffled forward. She bent over and peeked out the window once more. There, in front of her, was a grey skyline with not a tree in sight. Building after building dominated the horizon. Martha had never seen such a strange landscape. A wave of vertigo hit her, so she shut the curtains once more and went to sit on her bed.

It all seemed so surreal. She was hours from her home and in a very strange place. What's more, she was about to have dinner with Moses—just the two of them. Her heart pounded out of her chest, and she wiped the sweat from her brow with the back of her hand.

"*Nee*," she said aloud to herself. "You're not Amish any more. You're *Englisch* now. It's no use getting fanciful notions about Amish boys."

Still, Martha wondered how she could ever truly be *Englisch* when Moses Hostetler tugged ever so much at her heart.

Chapter Eight

It was a whole entire minute before Martha could reach across the bed and clasp the glass of water. She had awoken from her sleep with a sharp jolt after falling asleep, fully clothed, on the bed. All she had wanted to do was close her eyes for a few minutes.

Martha took a big sip of water as the unfamiliar objects in the room came into focus: the bedroom lamp, the strange artwork on the walls, and the television hanging above a desk which held a telephone.

Panic set in as Martha returned her glass to her nightstand and smoothed down her wild hair. She had to meet Moses at seven for dinner, and she had no idea what the time was now. What if it was already eight, and Moses had been knocking at the door and she hadn't heard him?

Stepping gingerly from bed, she crossed to the window and pulled back the curtains. It was not the rolling hills and the fields to which she was accustomed, the rolling hills and fields on which she had

played with her sisters as little girls. She half hoped
the sky outside would give her a clue as to the time,
but there was no way she could tell the time in this
strange place.

That was when Martha remembered her cell
phone. She almost laughed at herself for being so
silly. She hurried over to her purse and found it. It
was only six. Martha sighed with relief. She would
have time to get ready, as there was plenty of time to
have a shower and put on her make-up.

Martha allowed herself a small chuckle now. Back
home, if a woman was going on a buggy ride with a
man, she certainly didn't put on any make-up. Why,
there was not even a large mirror to be found in the
entire community. And tonight, Martha wouldn't be
wearing her dress, cape, and apron. No, she would
be wearing a black lace dress.

It was now that Martha shook off the small twinge
of guilt in her heart. She was on *rumspringa* and
could wear whatever she liked. She could even dress
like a Kardashian and nobody—or nothing—could
say a word, but still her heart would not allow her
to make such a decision. Her choice of dress for tonight was still extremely modest, by *Englisch* stan-
dards at any rate.

"But you are *Englisch* now," Martha said aloud.

As if to prove that to herself, she walked to the
bathroom and looked in the sparkling mirror. Her
long hair was even curlier now, no doubt because she
had tossed and turned when she slept on it. Sheryl
had told her it was the kind of hair girls used heat tools

to try to mimic, but to Martha, it was simply unruly. Maybe she should have borrowed the straightening iron after all, but Martha had no idea how to use it and would probably end up singeing her hair. She laughed aloud at the thought of turning up on her date with burned hair. Then she shuddered. Perhaps not.

Martha had a long, hot shower and then carefully pulled the dress over her shoulders. It was quite tight and she struggled with the zipper. Finally, she managed to get the zipper all the way to the top. Martha then looked at herself in the mirror again. To her dismay, the dress was above her knees, although only slightly. Also, it was a little too tight for her liking, but at least the sleeves were long and the neckline was high.

Martha went back to fetch the make-up. By now she had some practice with make-up and she didn't want to apply too much. For a minute, she wondered whether she should apply any, for her heart had just twinged a second time that night; make-up seemed too intense. Eventually she decided on a slight dusting of mineral powder and the new highlighter.

When Martha stood back to look at herself, she wondered if she had put on too much highlighter because her cheekbones were sparkling. "Maybe that's the way it's meant to look," Martha said to her reflection. She didn't need to apply mascara because her eyelashes were long and dark, so she simply brushed her eyebrows upward. She finished off the look with some clear lip gloss and then looked at the time on her cell phone once more.

It was almost seven. Martha had no idea where the time had gone.

Moments later, there was a knock on the door that caused Martha to drop her cell phone. That was when Martha finally saw a clock on her nightstand. She hadn't even noticed it before. She had been too overwhelmed by the thought of the date, and the dress and make-up she would be wearing. It was like the electric clock she had seen on Sheryl's nightstand. *Never mind that now*, Martha thought, as she snatched up her purse and hurried to the door as fast as she could in her wobbly heels.

"*Hiya*, Moses," she announced brightly as she stepped into the hall, but was taken aback by the look on his face. "What's wrong, Moses? You look like you've seen a ghost. Are you feeling well?"

"Yes, well, yes," Moses started. His eyebrows were practically soaring off his head. "You look…amazing!"

"*Denki*," Martha said, and then amended that to, "Thank you." Sheryl had told her to accept compliments graciously and that compliments were common amongst *Englischers*. Still, it was somewhat frowned upon to give compliments in her community, so she was shocked that Moses had given her one.

Martha stumbled in her heels as they walked toward the elevator, but she couldn't tell if that was because the heels really were extremely wobbly, or if it was because Moses continued to stare at her. "Stop staring at me, Moses," she scolded him. "Do I look too much like an *Englischer*?"

"You do look like an *Englischer*," Moses said, "but you are a very beautiful woman, Martha."

Martha was shocked that Moses had complimented her again. "*Nee*, you will make me prideful," she said. When she saw his face fall, she quickly added, "But thank you. It was lovely of you to say so."

Moses's face brightened again at once.

Martha had gone all warm and fuzzy inside at Moses's compliments. While she knew it was not good to be prideful, it made her wonder whether husbands and wives did complement each other in private. Maybe they did. She nodded to herself slowly.

"What's on your mind, Martha?" Moses said.

Martha was saved from responding when several people barged into the elevator. They avoided eye contact with Martha, which suited her just fine. She didn't want to make conversation with strangers, but on the other hand, she thought it strange how no one was particularly friendly.

"Are you hungry?" Moses asked her.

"Yes, I'm always hungry," Martha said. "Usually, I eat all day, but I haven't eaten since the train. I fell asleep in my room."

"So did I," Moses admitted.

"It's a good thing you woke up in time for dinner," Martha said.

"I set the alarm," Moses told her.

Martha was impressed. "Moses! How did you know how to do that?"

"Noah showed me when he was on *rumspringa*," Moses said and then flushed a startling red. Noah's *rumspringa* was an unpleasant memory for both the Hostetler and the Miller *familyes*.

Martha and Moses walked into the restaurant and Moses spoke to the man at the door. "Reservations for Moses Hostetler, for two," he said.

The man ushered them into the restaurant. Martha became uneasy when she saw several men turn to look at her. She figured Moses must have noticed too, because he stepped closer to her. Moses made her feel so much safer, and she was also glad that she was wearing a modest dress. She didn't know how *Englisch* girls dealt with being leered at like they were pieces of meat. None of the men who turned to look at her seemed like gentlemen.

Martha had hoped the restaurant would be fairly dark, like the one in which she'd had dinner with Gary, but this restaurant was quite bright. The lights above cast a pink glow over the myriad tables in the room. White starched tablecloths covered all the tables. The chairs at each table looked uncomfortable. They were a mustard color and were iron framed. There was no nook, booth, or even corner where anyone could sit and have a private conversation.

When they were seated, Martha looked around the room some more. "It's such a huge room," she said. "It's bigger than a huge barn inside."

"It is, indeed," Moses said.

"I feel like a fish in a goldfish bowl."

"*Jah*, I saw men looking at you when you came in." Moses was frowning as he spoke.

Is he jealous? Martha wondered. She was embarrassed at the thought, but despite herself, she was also a little pleased. This meant she wasn't watching her words. "It's very bright. I thought it would be dark. When I had dinner with Gary at a restaurant, it was much darker than this."

Moses's jaw fell open. "You had dinner with Gary?"

He sounds hurt, Martha thought. She quickly said, "It was just as friends. Sheryl told me…" She broke off. She was about to say that Sheryl told her to tell Gary they were having dinner just as friends.

"Oh, Sheryl told you to have dinner with Gary."

Martha did not respond. She did not want to mislead Moses, but he seemed a little upset. Perhaps it was better to let him think that. Besides, she didn't have dinner with Gary as a date. Still, if she were being honest with herself, she would have to admit it had been on her mind at the time. She had wanted to see what having a date with an *Englisch* man would be like.

Moses leaned forward. "Martha, are you all right? You look worried."

Martha shook her head. "I'm fine."

"You and Gary aren't dating or anything, are you?"

"No!" Martha exclaimed. "Of course not. Whatever would give you that idea?"

"You had dinner with him," he said.

"I'm having dinner with you and we're not dating." Martha regretted the words as soon as they were out of her mouth. Moses looked somewhat crestfallen and she felt bad. It wasn't what she meant to say. How could she be so hopeless with *menner*? She would need to get advice from someone. Perhaps Hannah could give her some sound advice.

The waiter arrived to ask if they were ready to order. They declined the wine menu and said they would need a little more time. There was a large blue bottle of water in the middle of the table, and Moses kindly poured some water for Martha.

As they studied the menu, and exclaimed over the unusual choices, the tension between them dissipated. "I think I'll have the Irish burger with Irish porter cheddar and fries, and then the hand-cut grilled Angus rib-eye steak for the main. It sounds *gut*, the mozzarella and Romano cheeses, and bacon bourbon jam. What about you, Martha?"

Martha decided to be adventurous. "I might try the cannelloni au gratin. I can't even picture it in my mind's eye, but the menu says it's a combination of beef and pork, flavored with porcini mushrooms rolled in a French crepe."

Moses nodded his approval. He had such a sweet face, Martha thought. "It does sound good. What about for the main?"

"The lemon sesame crusted chicken. It has whipped potatoes, honey roasted Brussels sprouts, and raspberry balsamic glaze," Martha said. "I'm particularly keen to try something chocolate for dessert later."

Moses chuckled. "Martha, did you ever think we'd be at a restaurant in New York having dinner, just the two of us?"

Martha laughed. "No, I didn't. Isn't it funny how things can happen when you least expect it?"

Martha and Moses ate their dinner in companionable silence. When the waiter gave them the dessert menus, Martha was delighted to see chocolate pecan pie on the menu. It was described as having chocolate ice cream, crème anglaise, and chocolate salted caramel sauce.

"It won't be as good as your chocolate cakes, Martha," Moses said.

Martha smiled at him. "Thank you for your support, Moses," she said.

"You always have my support," he began, and would have said more, but the waiter appeared at that moment to take the dessert orders.

"It's good," Martha said, after she'd sampled the chocolate pecan pie. "What do you think, Moses?"

"Yes, it is," he said, "but not as good as your baking, Martha."

She laughed. "Stop it, Moses. You'll make me prideful."

"Is there much preparation to be done for your meeting tomorrow?" Moses asked her.

"I've done all the preparation I can," Martha said. "I just need to remain calm and not say anything silly."

"Of course you won't say anything silly," Moses said. "You'll do very well."

"I hope the broker agrees to take me on as a client," Martha said, "or this whole trip will be wasted."

"It would not be wasted at all," Moses said softly, and he looked at her with warmth in his eyes.

Chapter Nine

Martha clutched her stomach as another wave of nausea hit her. She was sitting in the waiting room of the broker for several candy store franchises, waiting for her meeting, and it was already twenty minutes past her appointment time.

"You'll be fine," Moses said. His tone was reassuring, and it did offer Martha a small measure of relief. Still, the situation was daunting. Martha felt completely out of place and entirely foolish for even thinking the broker would be interested in anything she had to say.

Mercifully, the broker's offices were close enough to the motel to walk. It had been a long walk, and Martha suspected that an *Englischer* might have caught a cab. Nothing was going to make her catch a cab. She would rather walk five miles than even attempt to catch one.

The offices were even fancier than the motel. And while the receptionist had smiled at her, the smile did not reach her eyes. The woman's make-up was impeccable, and Martha had never seen anyone with such tightly stretched skin. Martha wondered what sort of herbs the woman applied to look like that. Her eyes were heavily made up and the blush on her cheeks was overpowering. She was impeccable in every way, even down to her impossibly long fingernails. *I bet she doesn't feed any chickens or chop any firewood with nails like that*, Martha thought.

The door opened, and Martha sat up straight. A tall, well-dressed woman hurried out. Her face was red and she brushed tears from her eyes. Martha caught her breath in alarm.

After a moment, the secretary looked up at her and said in a cold tone, "You may go in now."

Moses gave an encouraging nod. Martha walked into the large room showcasing the city skyline through expansive glass windows, but all she saw was the man sitting behind the desk. He exuded power and authority. His head was down, and he was making notes. He did not look up as Martha crossed the room to stand in front of him. She was entirely intimidated.

Finally he did look up, gave a cold, tight-lipped smile and stood up, extending his hand. "Miss Miller."

"Yes." Martha shook his hand. His grip was firm. His aftershave, smelling of vanilla, raisins, and cedarwood, was overpowering.

"I'm Rory Gauge. Please have a seat." He indicated the cold, hard desk chair opposite his desk.

Martha sat down, her stomach tight with nerves. Rory Gauge looked at his notes, and then up at Martha. "You wish to sell a range of handmade chocolates as a specialty item. Is that correct?" It sounded to Martha like an accusation.

"Yes." Martha tried to stop her knees from shaking.

"Tell me about them." He leaned back in his chair, and flicked a pen through his fingers, a look of concentration on his face.

Martha took a deep breath. "I do miniature shell molded pieces, and all sorts of chocolate coated products: butterscotch corn flake candy, butter crunch toffee, almond brittle, caramel pecans, cashew crunch, caramel candy, and my main one is the chocolate coated cherries. I have photos here." Martha opened the folder and handed the photos to Mr. Gauge. He took out a photo of a chocolate coated cherry, and stared at it for a while, turning it this way and that.

Martha pushed her feet into the ground to stop her knees from shaking.

After what seemed an age, Mr. Gauge looked up at her. "Very good." Martha smiled widely, but he continued. "They are well presented. They look good and I have no doubt they taste good. However,"—he waved his finger at Martha—"so do many chocolates on the market. What's your USP?"

Martha had been researching small businesses on Sheryl's computer, so knew a USP was a *Unique Selling Point*. She was prepared for this. "They are all genuine Amish chocolates."

Mr. Gauge leaned forward, his eyes glittering with interest. "They are all Amish recipes?"

Martha nodded. "Yes."

"And how did you come by Amish recipes?"

"I'm Amish."

Mr. Gauge narrowed his eyes. "You don't look Amish."

"I'm on *rumspringa*," Martha said. "Do you know what that is?" She hoped he wouldn't be offended by her question, and she also sent up small prayer of apology to *Gott* for her white lie for, while she was technically on *rumspringa*, she had no real intention of returning to the Amish.

Mr. Gauge did not appear offended at all. "Yes, I know what *rumspringa* is," he said. "So you're a real, genuine Amish person?"

Martha squirmed under his scrutiny, feeling like an exhibit in a museum. "Yes."

"You were brought up Amish? You have Amish parents and live on an Amish farm?"

Martha nodded. "Well, I was brought up Amish and have Amish parents, but my *daed* is a carpenter and has a furniture making business."

"And he's Amish?" Rory Gauge rubbed his hands together.

"Yes," Martha was a little put out as she'd already said that. She wondered where this conversation was going.

At once Mr. Gauge's whole demeanor changed. "Excellent," he exclaimed. "My clients don't have a line of Amish chocolates in our stores, and the tourists will love them." He rubbed his chin and looked over Martha's shoulder—she presumed at the wall—with a faraway look on his face.

"Are you attached to any particular name for your products, or if I offered you a contract, would you be prepared to listen to my suggestions for a name?"

Martha tried not to show her excitement. "Yes, I'd be prepared to listen to names," she said as evenly as she could, when all she wanted to do was scream with delight and jump up and down with excitement.

"And I'll want to have professional photos taken of you in full Amish costume for marketing purposes."

Martha winced at the word *costume*, but spoke up. "Amish don't believe in having their faces photographed."

Rory Gauge rubbed his chin again. "Ah, I see. Is there a known Amish symbol that we could use instead on the packaging?"

Martha shook her head.

"What about a model dressed in an Amish costume?"

Martha did her best not to wince again. "Yes, that would be fine." She was relieved that the photo issue wasn't going to be a deal breaker. She realized all at once that she was no longer an Amish person; she was becoming an *Englischer*. Why had said she was Amish? *Maybe it was force of habit*, she thought.

"All right then, I'll set up a meeting with the buyer and we'll go through the figures and the supply numbers, but if that all works out, Miss Miller, you have yourself a deal."

Martha stood up and shook Mr. Gauge's hand. She

could not believe how blessed she was to land a contract for her handmade chocolates. Well, there was no signed contract yet, but there soon would be.

Martha was on cloud nine. The powerful Rory Gauge had thought her chocolates had merit, and all being well, she would soon sign a contract to supply his stores with specialty chocolates. Her chocolate business was well on its way. It was beyond her wildest dreams.

Chapter Ten

Martha arrived home from work in a fluster. She had felt overheated all day, and hoped she wasn't coming down with something. Mr. Gauge had sent her a contract to sign, and so her business was now officially on its way.

Martha made herself a nice cup of meadow tea. Sheryl wasn't home, so she tried to call Moses that the contract had arrived. She was bursting to tell someone the good news. The Hostetlers had a phone in their main barn, but it rang out three times. Martha sat down on the couch and sipped her meadow tea. She felt dejected. Sure, she should have been elated, but she was used to having a whole community to share her triumphs and her disappointments. Now, she had no one at all with whom to share her good news. Martha had just found another drawback to being *Englisch*.

Martha did not want to call Moses's *mudder* at her quilt store and tell her. That could be awkward. She had, however, called her *daed's* business and told him, and he had seemed genuinely pleased for her and said he'd pass the news onto her *mudder* and her *schweschder* Rebecca, and to Noah to tell Hannah, Jacob and Esther, and Moses. Martha wasn't sure her own *mudder* would be too happy about her news, but speaking to her *daed* had left her feeling awfully homesick.

Martha decided to make meat loaf with glazed ketchup over bacon strips for dinner. While she herself wasn't particularly hungry, Sheryl always returned home after work in a ravenous state. Martha changed from her work clothes into jeans and a tee, all the while thinking that jeans were uncomfortable and wishing for her Amish dresses, and then groaned when she reached the kitchen. Sheryl had obviously been home earlier and had left a mess. There was an empty box of fried pork chop and gravy next to a plate that had most of the gravy and cheese-topped, mashed potatoes still on it. An empty and half crushed can of soda lay next to it.

Martha sighed and threw the can and the box in the trash, and then scraped the remainder of the food down the garbage disposal with a fork. What happened next, Martha had no idea, for suddenly the fork flew into the garbage disposal unit. The garbage disposal made a horrible, whirring sound, so Martha hurriedly turned off the garbage disposal at the wall switch.

She had been feeling hot before, but now her blood ran cold. Sheryl was generous with everything, her clothes, her jewelry, her make-up, and was quite laid back in nature, but the one thing she was obsessed with, was the garbage disposal unit. She was always offering dire warnings: *Don't put pasta or rice down the unit*; *don't put potato peels down the unit*; *don't put chicken bones down the unit*.

Even the other day, Sheryl had wagged her finger at Martha and said, "Don't put coffee grinds down the garbage disposal, no matter what anyone tells you. People say it's fine, but it is *not*."

It was a wonder Martha had ever been brave enough to use the garbage disposal at all, but lately she had been, although she drew the line at using the dishwasher. She was in the habit of taking everything out of the dishwasher and washing it in the sink. It's just that the garbage disposal made it easy to clean up after Sheryl.

Now Martha stood there, her hands to her cheeks, horrified that she seemed to have broken the garbage disposal unit. It was her fault, so she couldn't call the property manager and ask her to send a plumber. She herself couldn't afford a plumber. What would she do?

Martha picked up her cell phone and called the Hostetler barn. No one had answered all week, but she just had to try. Again no answer, so she tried one more time. This time Elijah answered. "Elijah, it's Martha Miller. Is Moses around?"

"Yes, I'll go get him."

A few minutes passed and then Moses spoke. "*Hiya*, Martha."

"*Hiya*, Moses. I have great news. I've signed the contract for the chocolates."

"*Wunderbar*!" Moses sounded genuinely pleased. After an interval, he asked, "Martha, is something wrong?"

"Yes, as a matter of fact. I've broken Sheryl's garbage disposal unit. I dropped a fork down there, and…"

Moses interrupted. "Did you turn it off?"

"Yes, of course."

"I'll be right there. Don't touch it, whatever you do." Moses hung up.

Martha rubbed her hands together anxiously. Did Moses know anything about garbage disposal units? Sure, he was handy, but did he know anything about electricity? His *mudder* had electricity in her quilt store, but she was unlikely to have a garbage disposal unit there, and even if she did, she had probably never thrown a fork into it.

Martha sat on the sofa, feeling sorry for herself. What if Moses hadn't answered when she'd called the Hostetler barn? Sheryl would have come home and no doubt would have been angry with her that she had broken the garbage disposal unit. Well, that could still happen, Martha thought, but she was relieved that Moses was coming to her rescue. No matter what happened, she would be all the better for Moses's presence. She felt all alone in the *Englisch* world, without her support network that she had always taken for granted.

It seemed like an age before Moses knocked on the door, and Martha was overcome with joy to see him.

Moses frowned. "Why are you looking at me like that, Martha?"

"I'm just so pleased to see you."

Moses beamed. "Well, show me to the problem."

Martha laughed. "You sound just like a plumber."

Moses chuckled too. "Not really, because I'm free."

Martha thought for a moment about the Amish, how they always help their neighbors, and what a wide support network there is within the community. She wondered how *Englischers* managed to get on, as they were not so community oriented.

Moses leaned under the sink and unplugged the disposal. "Martha, can you pass me that quarter inch hex key please?"

Martha simply said, "Umm," while looking through the tools, so Moses popped out from under the sink and retrieved the tool. He then disappeared back under the sink.

Martha peeped in. "What are you doing?"

"I'm rotating the hex key clockwise and counter clockwise to try to release the fork."

Martha was impressed. "Sounds like you know what you're doing."

"Hmmpf," was the muffled reply.

"Is it working?" Martha was anxious. "Sheryl will be home soon."

Moses popped out from under the unit and stood up, holding a mangled fork.

"Oh, Moses!" Martha flung her arms around his

neck without thinking, and then jumped back, hugely embarrassed. Sheryl was always hugging her, Gary, and everyone else who came in the flat, and Martha had picked up the habit. Yet Amish weren't likely to show affection in public, and she was beside herself that she had hugged Moses.

Martha stared at Moses, trying to determine his reaction, but he simply looked surprised. "Sorry, I've become an *Englischer*." Martha forced a laugh, trying to cover up what she had just done.

"I'm not complaining, Martha. Hug me all you like." Moses winked at her.

It was Martha's turn to be surprised. *Is he flirting with me?* she wondered. The two of them locked eyes, and a strange feeling ran through Martha. She wanted to look away, but was unable to do so.

Just then, Sheryl burst through the door, dragging two large bags, both adorned with an interlocking *G*, into her apartment. "Hi, Moses, Martha." She hurried straight past them into her bedroom.

"Quick, the tools," Martha said in a low tone. She and Moses went to the kitchen and packed away his tools. Moses turned on the water in the sink and fiddled with some switches, and then said, "It's working fine now."

"How did you know how to fix it, Moses? It's electric and all. How did you know what to do?"

Moses leaned close to Martha and said in a conspiratorial tone, "It's one of my secrets. I have lots of secrets, Martha."

Martha suddenly felt anxious. Her palms felt

sweaty and she wiped them on her jeans. *Secrets?* Could Moses mean he was dating Laura? Laura hadn't said so, and she talked about Moses a lot, but then she also talked about Gary. What secrets did Moses have that Martha didn't know about?

Chapter Eleven

Martha came home after a hard morning's work at the café. She was a little shaken because she had confessed to Ava, the café's owner, that she didn't have any qualifications. To her delight, Ava did not mind at all. Martha had been careful to explain that she hadn't known what qualifications were at the time, and that she had thought she was qualified because she was experienced with baking the type of cakes that the café wanted.

Martha thought Ava would be angry or maybe even fire her, but Ava seemed to take it with a grain of salt. She told Martha she was delighted with the cakes and pastries she made and wanted her to make more of the chocolate triple layer cakes.

Martha was relieved but a little guilty she hadn't told Ava sooner. Also, it was rather stressful baking in a commercial situation. Back at home, although she sometimes had to cook for many people, there was no pressure. It was in the peace and quiet of her family kitchen rather than in the hustle and bustle of a busy café kitchen with people calling out orders and rushing to and fro.

Martha kicked off her shoes and threw herself down on a couch. She stretched her arms behind her. She realized she hadn't had lunch, but Mary was coming to visit today and she wanted to have lunch with her. Still, Martha was hungry, so she went to the kitchen wondering what light snacks she could have. Before she got the opportunity to find any snacks, there was a knock on the door.

Martha hurried over to the door. "Mary," she explained with delight. "Come in."

"How did you get here, by the way?"

"Your mother gave me money for a taxi."

Martha could barely suppress a shudder. She still thought of people pushing others out of the way to get to the yellow cabs in New York.

"Is something wrong, Martha?" Mary asked her.

"No, not at all," Mary said. "I was just thinking of New York."

Mary beamed. "Congratulations! I heard you did very well. You even have a contract."

"I don't think my mother is too happy about it," Martha confessed.

Mary nodded. "I think she was worried about you going to New York, especially that you didn't tell them you were going."

Martha sat on the couch and rubbed her hand over her eyes. "I guess something else I have to feel guilty about, I suppose."

"What's the other thing?" Mary asked.

Martha smiled to herself. She knew Mary must be relaxed, because she wasn't chattering away. "Just a work thing. Nothing much," she said with a dismissive wave of her hand. "I'll heat up our lunch. I prepared it last night. It's an Italian dish called risotto," Martha added, "and then we can have some of my chocolate. What did you want to talk with me about?"

Mary shifted from one foot to the other and avoided Martha's gaze. "Can I tell you over lunch? I always feel calmer when I'm eating. This matter is making me quite nervous. I don't know why it's making me nervous, but it is. Well, of course I know why it's making me nervous. It's embarrassing. That's why I don't want to tell anyone else. I could have told Esther, but she's so sick with the morning sickness and all, so I have no one to talk to but you. You don't mind, do you?"

Martha smiled. It was clear to her Martha was nervous now. "Of course I don't mind. Let's eat."

Soon the two of them were sitting at the little dining table, eating their food. Mary pushed her food around her plate with her fork.

"Out with it, Mary," Martha said. "You'll feel better once you tell me."

Mary's face fell. "It's about David."

"David?" Martha said, wondering whether this conversation was going.

"Yes, David. It's embarrassing. I don't know how to tell you."

"You like him, don't you?"

Mary looked shocked. "Is it obvious? Please tell me it's not obvious. I hope I haven't embarrassed myself in front of David, making it so obvious to him that I like him."

"Of course it is not obvious," Martha said. "You said it was about David. So really, what else could it be?"

Mary appeared to be considering her words. "I see. *Jah*, I like David." She spoke in a lowered voice and then looked around the room.

Martha frowned. "We're the only ones here."

Mary nodded. "I really like him, but he doesn't like me."

"What makes you think that?" Martha asked her.

Mary held up both hands, palms upward. "It's obvious, isn't it? He hasn't asked me on a buggy ride. It's obvious he sees me just as a friend."

"But you two have such a good time together, and you have that common bond over Pirate. You're always having a good time with David and Pirate."

Mary was eating food and waited until she finished her mouthful before speaking. She swallowed loudly. "That's just the problem. We have a good time just like good friends. He doesn't see me as a woman. He just sees me as a friend."

Martha wasn't so sure about that. She had suspected from time to time that David was interested in Mary. "Perhaps that's what David thinks about you. Perhaps he thinks *you* only see him as a friend."

Mary looked doubtful.

"Is he seeing a girl at the moment?"

Mary shook her head. "*Nee*. Not as far as I know, anyway."

Martha leaned forward. "Well then, has he taken a girl home after a Singing? Or has he ever seemed interested in any girls at Singing?"

Mary looked at the ceiling and bit her lip. "*Nee*. Abigail Eicher keeps following him around, trying to talk to him, but he doesn't seem interested. He keeps walking away."

"All that is surely good, isn't it?" Martha asked her.

Mary stabbed a piece of chicken with her fork. "No, it's not good, because he hasn't asked me on a buggy ride. If he liked me, he would ask me on a buggy ride. It's that simple. I don't think he likes any girls in our community. Maybe he's writing to a girl in another community. *Nee*, Martha, I'm sure he only sees me as a friend."

Martha was at a loss. She had no idea how to respond. She was worried that David might still be seeing *Englisch* girls. She thought she had better tell Mary about his past. "Um, Mary," Martha began, wondering how to break it to her gently, "David used to, um, well…"

Mary finished her sentence for her. "Hannah saw David with an *Englisch* girl once. They were kissing in public."

Martha gasped. "You knew?"

"*Jah*. Hannah told me. Anyway, David told me he used to run around with *Englisch* girls but said that was when he was young and silly. He feels bad about it now."

This is getting stranger and stranger, Martha thought. Aloud she said, "David discussed it with you?" Before Mary had a chance to respond, Martha added, "Surely he must like you, in that case. Why else would he say such a personal thing to you?"

"Because he sees me as friend," Mary lamented. "He probably doesn't even realize I'm a woman! What can I do?"

"I don't know," Martha admitted. "I don't really know what you can do. And you're sure he only sees you as a friend? Are you absolutely positive?"

Mary nodded slowly, a sad expression on her face. "Yes, I'm sure."

"And you're not interested in any other boys?"

Mary's expression brightened. "I see! You're saying I should make him jealous."

Martha waved her left hand at Mary. "*Nee, nee, nee.* That wasn't what I was saying at all."

A knock at the door interrupted their conversation. Martha went to open it.

"Gary," she said. He was standing next to a little boy. Martha guessed the boy to be around the age of eight.

"This is my little brother, Sam," Gary announced.

Sam walked into the room, scratching his arm. "My clothes are itchy," he said to no one in particular. He was carrying a stick.

"What's the stick for?" Martha asked Gary in lowered tones.

"Sam likes to collect rocks and unusually shaped

sticks," Gary said. "He's pretty much obsessed with them. That's because he's on the autism spectrum."

"I see."

Sam sat opposite Mary. "Would the two of you like some lunch, Gary?" Martha asked him. "I have plenty."

"Yes, I was hoping you'd say that," Gary admitted. "That's why I brought Sam over here. I have nothing in my fridge at all. Our mother has a really bad case of flu, so I'm minding Sam for a few days."

"This is my friend, Mary," Martha said, "and Mary, this is Gary. He lives in the building."

Gary hurried over to Mary and stuck out his hand to shake hers, but then pulled his hand back swiftly. "Oh, I'm sorry."

Mary looked confused. "What for?"

"I mean, do you Amish shake hands? I don't know anything about the Amish."

"But what about Martha?" Mary said. "She's Amish."

"Martha is not Amish anymore," Gary said, his words earning a gasp from Mary.

"Sure we shake hands," Mary said, and the two of them shook hands.

"Come to think of it, don't you have a secret handshake or something?" Gary asked. He planted his palm on his forehead. "Silly me. That's the Freemasons, isn't it?"

Martha and Mary exchanged glances. "I'll fetch you some lunch," Martha said.

Mary rose to help her, but Martha waved her back

down. When Martha reached the kitchen, she considered perhaps Mary wanted to help her to escape from Gary. He did seem a little strange at times.

By the time Martha returned to the table with two steaming plates of food, which she deposited in front of Sam and Gary, she was relieved to see Mary and Gary chatting happily away.

Mary had already finished her dinner. Martha had finished hers too so they sat and waited for Sam and Gary to finish.

"What's that?" Mary said, pointing to Sam's stick. He was twirling it around with one hand, and eating with the other.

He handed it to her. "It's my favorite stick."

She inspected the stick. "It's a very good stick. I throw sticks to my dog, but not nice sticks like this, only ordinary sticks."

"You have a dog?" Martha noted that Sam avoided eye contact with Mary.

"Yes I do," she said. "He's a very tall dog." She handed the stick back.

Sam continued to eat while twirling the stick.

"So are you and Martha from the same religious group?" Gary asked Mary.

Mary giggled. "It's not a religious group. I think you mean a community." When Gary looked blank, she pushed on. "When Martha and her sisters were in the buggy accident, their bishop was friends with our bishop and he asked our bishop for someone to go and help the Millers because all the girls had injuries. So I went to help Mrs. Miller and I liked it so much there, that I haven't gone home. I mean, I visited home several times, but I haven't gone home to live."

"What's it like being Amish?" Gary asked her.

Mary raised her eyebrows. "Haven't you asked Martha that?"

Gary narrowed his eyes. "I don't really think of Martha as Amish. Maybe it's because she doesn't dress in Amish cloths."

Mary nodded. "Yes, but it's not what's on the outside of someone that counts, but what's on the inside them."

Gary nodded solemnly. "Quite so, quite so. You're quite wise for your age, young Mary."

"I'm definitely not much younger than you."

Gary laughed. "Don't worry, I won't ask how old you are. I know better than to ask a lady her age." To Sam, he said, "Are you having a good time?"

Sam nodded.

"How about some ice cream and chocolate?" Martha said.

Sam seemed quite pleased by the suggestion, as did Gary. This time, Mary helped Martha in the kitchen. "He seems nice," Mary whispered to Martha. "Does he have a girlfriend?"

"Not as far as I know," Martha said. "You're not going to try to make David jealous, are you?" She looked up, but Mary was already heading out of the kitchen. Martha sighed and followed her.

"My mother was taking Sam camping this weekend, but now she's got the flu," Gary said.

"That's too bad," Martha said. "Maybe you can go again soon as your mother's better."

Gary shook his head. "No, it's all arranged. I'm going to take him camping for the weekend. Martha, I was hoping you, Sheryl, and Laura could come with me. It's all paid for already, paid in full."

"Camping?" Martha said with alarm. She had never been camping and said so.

Gary waved one hand at her in dismissal. "There's nothing to it, truly. I wouldn't worry about it, if I were you. You just pitch a tent and build a campfire and then sit around playing board games or telling funny stories. I always play the guitar."

It sounded quite boring to Martha, but she plastered a smile on her face. "Yes, lots of people seem to enjoy camping." Some *familyes* in her community had been camping, but the Millers never had.

"I was hoping you could all come with me to help look after Sam," Gary said. "It's just for one night." Martha could sense the desperation in his voice. Her heart went out to him. She didn't think Gary was the most responsible person in the world, and he was taking his little brother away camping. "If Sheryl goes, I'll go too," Martha said.

"That sounds wonderful," Gary said. "What about you, Mary?"

"I have to help Mrs. Miller," she said, "but thanks for asking."

Mary kept staring at Gary. Martha didn't know if she was genuinely interested in him or whether she was simply keen to be having a long conversation with an *Englischer.* One thing was clear, Sam seemed taken with Mary. He showed her the stick at intervals, and Mary continued to exclaim over it, which made Sam's face light up.

Sheryl burst through the door, clutching several bags. "Hello, everyone," she said. She practically ran past them to go to her bedroom.

A minute or so later, she came out and sat at the table.

"Sheryl, this is my friend Mary, from back home."

Mary must have been nervous to have two *Englischers* is in the one room because she spoke rapidly. "Yes, I haven't known Martha for very long, but I've known her for some time. Martha and I are friends. I'm also friends with her sisters. I live in the *grossmammi haus* behind the Millers' house. I enjoy living by myself. Someone else once stayed with me for a while when her house burned down, but then she left because everyone rebuilt her house. Oh sorry, I'm talking too much, aren't I?" She put her hand over her mouth, but soon took it away. "Just tell me if I'm talking too much," she added.

"Would you like some lunch?" Martha asked Sheryl as soon as Mary stopped talking.

"Maybe later," Sheryl said. "I've just had lunch and I'm quite full. Hi, Sam."

Sam did not acknowledge her.

"I have a big favor to ask you, Sheryl," Gary said. "I've already asked Martha and she said she would if you would."

Martha wasn't happy to put on the spot like that.

"What is it?" Sheryl asked, looking between the two of them.

"My mother's come down with a bad case of flu, so Sam has to stay with me for the weekend. Mom had already promised to take him camping, but obviously she can't go now, so I said I'd take him."

"Camping? How long for?" Sheryl's tone was wary.

"Just overnight on Saturday night," Gary said. "Come on, Sheryl, it will be fun. I was hoping Laura could come too."

"Sure, why not."

The relief on Gary's face was unmistakable.

"But what supplies will we need?" Sheryl asked. "We'll need tents and sleeping bags. No wait, maybe we need airbeds and a pump, so we won't have to sleep on the hard ground. And what about a portable propane gas barbecue?"

"A campfire will be fine," Gary said. "There are fire rings on site. I've got plenty of camping gear and air beds. Before the divorce, my parents used to go camping all the time, and Mom's got a lot of camping gear. You won't need anything, seriously, only camping clothes."

"I don't have any camping clothes," Martha said.

Sheryl shot her a speculative look. "I'll go out and get you some this afternoon. I'll have to get myself some too."

"I'll come and buy some for myself," Martha said.

Sheryl wouldn't hear a word of it. "No, I insist. I absolutely insist."

Martha didn't like the idea of Sheryl paying for her

clothes. She figured she would go with her and offer to pay for the clothes when they reached the stores. "I'll go shopping with you."

"No you won't," Sheryl said. "I enjoy shopping. It's my downtime and I find it relaxing. I only find relaxing and fun when I'm by myself though. So what clothes will you need?" She scratched her head.

"Just casual clothes, of course," Gary said, "and socks and good walking boots. That's all. I'll bring everything else. I have plenty of airbeds and a pump. I've got all the camping gear—you just need to bring yourselves."

"We'll need to bring food," said the ever-practical Martha.

"We'll just take cans of food and heat them in a pot over the fire," Gary said.

Martha wrinkled her nose.

"And we can have s'mores," Sheryl said with delight.

"S'mores," Sam repeated.

"Do you like s'mores?" Mary asked him.

He nodded. Martha noted that he didn't make eye contact with anyone, and he seemed a little socially awkward, but then he was only eight years old.

"Well, that's settled," Gary said with delight. "Who's going to ask Laura?"

"You can ask her," Sheryl said. "Why don't you go and ask her now. Is she is working this afternoon, Martha?"

Martha said that she was.

Sheryl shooed Gary out of the apartment. "Off you

go. Go ask her now and Sam can stay with us. That is, if Sam doesn't mind?"

"Maybe I should give him some chocolates first," Martha said.

Sam seemed quite happy to eat chocolate ice cream and salted caramel candies while Gary hurried to the café to invite Laura.

Sheryl was clearly enthusiastic about camping. "Isn't this exciting! Have you been camping before, Martha?" Without waiting for Martha to respond, she added, "I love camping. It's such fun. We'll have so much fun, you'll see!"

Chapter Twelve

Martha awoke before the first rays of sun. She tossed and turned. She didn't want to get up and make herself coffee in case she woke Sheryl. Today was the day they were going camping. Martha considered she'd had a little bit too much excitement lately with the trip to New York. Sure, she had gained a chocolate contract, and that was what she had wanted. However, she didn't feel as though she could go back to New York ever again. She also wasn't sure about camping.

Martha had followed the same pattern since she was born, and now in a few short weeks of *rumspringa* her world had been turned upside down. She was beginning to crave the stability of her familiar surroundings. What's more, she missed Moses. She hadn't seen him for a while and she wondered what he was doing.

Mary had told her that Abigail Eicher was interested in David, but Martha knew that Abigail had always had eyes for Moses. Was that why she hadn't heard from Moses? Was it because he was interested in Abigail? Or someone else?

Moses's mother's store was not too far from Martha's apartment and Moses could easily visit if he wanted. Obviously he didn't want to visit her.

Martha sat up and then lay back down. She tossed and turned, willing herself back to sleep. It did not work. Martha's thoughts turned to Sam. She had seen more of him in the past day. He had shown her his stick collection and some of his rocks. He was a delightful boy. Martha wondered what her own son would look like. Would he look like Sam? Sam was tall for his age, and Moses was tall.

Martha sat bolt upright. Moses? Why did her mind follow that train of thought? Maybe she was overtired.

Martha laid back down and put the pillow over her head in the hopes she could go back to sleep if it was dark. That didn't work, so after half an hour Martha got up and tiptoed into the kitchen. She looked at the coffee machine. It made a loud sound when it was turned on, and she didn't want to wake Sheryl. Still, she faced this decision every morning and usually ended up making the coffee. Sometimes Sheryl woke and sometimes she didn't. But even if the noise of the coffee machine did wake her, Sheryl never seemed to mind. Or maybe she was just being polite. Martha shrugged and turned on the coffee machine.

Martha was sitting alone at the table eating toast and drinking coffee. She had never once eaten alone before she had become *Englisch*. It seemed strange and she didn't like it. "Am I having second thoughts about being *Englisch*?" Martha said quietly to herself.

"What did you say?" Sheryl said.

"Oh, sorry, I didn't even see you come out of your bedroom. I didn't wake you, did I?"

"No. I thought Gary said we were going to get an early start."

"He did?"

Sheryl laughed. "Silly me. I forgot to tell you. Anyway, did you like the clothes I bought you?"

Martha was once embarrassed. "Yes, but, Sheryl, you must allow me to pay for them."

Sheryl held up both hands in front of her. "No way! It's kind of you to help Gary with Sam. We're both doing him a favor, so I wouldn't want you to have to pay."

Martha scratched her head, thinking how easy it was to scratch her head when there was no prayer *kapp* or bonnet in the way. "But we're doing Gary a favor. I'm not doing you a favor."

Sheryl laughed. "Don't be so confusing before I have caffeine." She disappeared into the kitchen and then returned with a mug of coffee. "When you fell asleep while watching TV the other night there was a show on about Amish people."

Martha was intrigued. "There was? I missed it."

"Never mind. It will be back on soon. Anyway, there was a man who ate coffee soup. Have you ever heard of it?"

"I know Mary likes coffee oats," Martha said, "but I don't like it. Some people in the community eat coffee soup. They break up toast or crackers into a bowl and then pour coffee over it along with cream and sugar. Some people even put potatoes and cheese in it."

Sheryl pulled an expression of distaste. "Eek! That sounds absolutely disgusting."

Martha chuckled. "I've never had it. It doesn't sound too nice, but it might surprise you."

"I won't be trying it," Sheryl said over her shoulder as she hurried to answer a knock on the door.

Gary and Sam walked in. Sam was twirling a stick between his fingers.

"Are you excited to be going camping?" Martha asked him.

Sam nodded but did not meet her eyes.

"Are you ready to go now?" Gary said. "We haven't had breakfast, by the way. If you want to take that as hint, it is."

Sheryl waved them over to the table. "Would you like coffee?"

"Sam's too young!" Gary said in fright.

Sheryl rolled her eyes. "Honestly, Gary! I meant for you. I'll give you both toast."

"I've been meaning to buy eggs and bacon," Martha said. "How have you been going with cooking for Sam?"

"We've been getting takeout," Gary said.

Gary must have been ravenous as he ate five pieces of toast in quick succession. Sam seemed too busy twirling his stick to eat much, which made Martha a little concerned. "Gary, can I get Sam something else to eat?"

"We'll get him something on the way to the campground," Gary said. He seemed a little distracted.

"Laura is still coming, isn't she?" Martha asked him.

"Yes, we'll swing by her house next."

Gary spent a long time eating, and asked for ice cream as well. Sam, too, seemed hungry. So much for the early start—they waited at Laura's apartment for an hour for her to get ready.

It was late morning before they were on their way to the campground. Martha wondered what camping would be like. Part of her was looking forward to the new experience, and part of her wanted to go home and see her family. *Just a little visit*, she thought. *Maybe I could visit my family once a week.*

Laura sighed. "I'm not sure about camping. I don't like getting dirty."

Gary looked across at her. She was in sitting next to him, while Martha and Sheryl were in the back seat with Sam sitting between them.

"You're doing me a favor, Laura," Gary said. "Thanks."

"You weren't joking when you said they had bathrooms, were you?" she asked him.

He hurried to reassure her. "Of course not. They have nice, clean bathrooms. I've been there before. If you don't believe me, go to their website and check out the reviews. Mom wouldn't take Sam camping somewhere where they didn't have good facilities."

"It's a shame they don't have cabins," Laura added.

"They *do* have cabins," Gary said, "but we always have more fun in an actual tent. What fun is a cabin?"

Laura leaned over to the back seat and wriggled her eyebrows at Martha and Sheryl.

Martha figured that camping couldn't be all that bad. After all, she was used to plain living, and Gary even said there were airbeds. How hard could it be? She just didn't want to sit around idly. She would rather be doing something. Besides, there was her chocolate business to plan, but Gary certainly did need help with Sam and she could hardly begrudge him her time. Gary seemed quite absent-minded and Martha didn't think he was the most suitable person to mind a young child.

The drive to the camping grounds was not far, much to Martha's relief. "You might see a deer," Gary said to Sam. To the women, Gary said, "Sam loves animals."

"Mary said you should take him out to see her dog, Pirate, one day," Martha said.

"Already discussed," Gary said.

Martha gasped. "It is?" She wondered when that had happened. She certainly hoped Mary wasn't going to try to make David jealous. Martha would have asked Gary more, but he was already out of the car and heading over to the office.

"The area is more wooded than I thought," Laura said with dismay. "I thought we would be camping on rolling fields and not stuck in the woods. I wonder how big the tents are?"

That was the first question she asked Gary when he returned to the car. "You'll soon see," he said.

"Put me out of my misery," Laura said. "I'd rather know now."

"Sam and I have a two-person dome tent, and the three of you have a big four person tent," he said. "They won't take long to pitch."

"I went camping when I was a child," Laura said, "and the tent took ages to pitch and then it fell down."

Gary shook his head. "Tents are much better these days. You'll see!"

Martha wondered how she would feel camping for so many hours. She had brought along Dutch Blitz and was planning to show them how to play it. Sheryl had brought Scrabble. Martha had also brought along pen and paper in case she had ideas about her chocolate business. She doubted she would have, but she did not want to be unprepared.

Gary drove off. They drove past RV's, campers, and cabins, and then came to a heavily wooded area. "Is it much further?" Laura asked him. "Aren't we too far from the bathrooms now?"

"No, we're not that far at all," Gary said. "Anyways, we're here now." He pulled into an area next to a picnic table. "See! There's method in my madness," he said. "We don't need a camping table, because this table is already here. We'll camp here and we're not far from the stream either, so we'll have fresh water."

Gary jumped out of the car and within two strides was at the trunk. Martha wondered where he got his energy. He was always rushing around, whereas the

Amish always did things deliberately and some would say, slowly. On the other hand, Gary was always in a hurry, but he never did seem to get much done.

Gary had put all the parts of the tents on the ground when Martha noticed Sam was still in the car. "Do you want to get out of the car?" she asked him, but he did not look at her and continued to wave the stick in a set pattern. "Would you like to come out and find more interesting sticks and rocks?" she asked him.

Sam slid across the seat.

"Unless you need help with the tents, Sam and I going looking for sticks and rocks," Martha told Gary.

"That's great. Thanks, Martha. No, I don't need anyone's help. I can get these tents up by myself."

Laura and Sheryl exchanged glances, while Martha and Sam went off to explore and look at sticks and rocks.

Martha thought she would have trouble finding interesting sticks, but found plenty around a fallen tree. Sam seemed quite excited, although proved to be quite fussy when selecting sticks. In the end, he only selected five small sticks. Martha offered to help him carry them, but he wanted to carry them himself.

When they got back, the tents were up. There was a big red tent and a smaller yellow tent. The red tent was much better than Martha had expected.

Martha was impressed. Still, she couldn't shake off the uneasy feeling that something bad was going to happen.

Chapter Thirteen

"Gary, did you forget the food?" Sheryl asked, looking in the trunk of the car.

"Of course not. I've already unpacked it."

Laura tapped his arm in a flirtatious manner. "Always have things under control, don't you, Gary."

Gary looked quite pleased. "What should we do next?" Sheryl asked him.

"I've been camping for years," he said. "Let's get organized and then I'll start the fire."

The girls pumped up their airbeds in turn. Martha was surprised at the amount of clothes and supplies the other two women had brought. They each had a huge supply of make-up, and various shoes and different sorts of clothes. Sheryl had even brought her curling wand.

Martha sat on her airbed and was surprised how comfortable it was, but both Sheryl and Laura complained. "It's not quite the same as a nice comfy bed at home, is it?" Sheryl said, and Laura agreed with her.

"At least the tent floor is lined," Sheryl continued. "No chance of bugs getting in and biting us."

Laura pulled a face. "No mirrors, though. I only have this one." She pulled a small mirror from her purse. "Martha, Amish aren't allowed to have mirrors, is that right?"

Martha laughed. "Yes, we just don't have big mirrors in our community."

Both Sheryl and Laura looked horror-stricken. "What, what? No mirrors at all?" Sheryl sputtered.

"Yes, we have mirrors. The men need them to shave. We just don't have big mirrors."

"Why don't you have big mirrors?" Laura asked her.

"It would encourage vanity," Martha said.

"Don't tell me you've never looked at your reflection in a steel pot," Sheryl said, shaking her finger at her. "I know that's what I'd do. Or maybe in a pond."

Martha joined in the laughter.

"It's going to be hard for you to go home, now that you're used to big mirrors," Laura said.

"I'm not going home. I'm staying *Englisch*," Martha said, and then clamped her hand over her mouth.

Sheryl raised her eyebrows. "You are?"

Martha shrugged one shoulder. "I haven't made up my mind yet. I don't really know what I'm doing."

"Knock, knock," Gary called from outside the tent.

"The tent flap is open," Sheryl said.

"Yes, but I couldn't knock, and I wanted to be polite. Will I light the fire now? Sam would like some s'mores."

The women followed him to the to the fire ring. "I'll just fetch some kindling," Martha said.

Gary shot her an appraising look. "Oh yes, you'd be quite used to fires, wouldn't you?"

Before Martha could respond, he had stacked large pieces of wood on the fire.

"No, you need to start with kindling," Martha said, concerned. "That will never catch light."

"I've been camping for years," Gary told her. "You don't have to be like a Boy Scout rubbing two sticks together. This is the fastest way. Sam, stand back."

Sam was already a long way from the fire, twirling a stick around his fingers. Gary waved a box of fire starter cubes at Martha. "This is the fastest way to get a fire going." He wedged the entire box of fire starter cubes under the logs and then picked up a bottle.

"What's that?" Laura asked him.

"Denatured alcohol." With that, he tipped one quarter of a bottle over the logs.

"Stand back," he said. When he saw that everyone had stepped back, he flicked a match onto the fire.

Boom! It went up with a bang. Martha was at once concerned for Sam, but he did not appear to mind. She figured that this must be Gary's usual way of lighting fires when they went camping. "Gary, that's incredibly dangerous," she scolded him. "Please promise me you'll never do that again."

"I can't promise that," Gary said with a laugh. "How long would it take you to light a fire?"

"Not long with some kindling," Martha said.

"How long would it take you to get the fire to this extent with just kindling?"

Martha crossed her arms over her chest. Gary clearly wasn't going to listen to her and he had just lit the fire in a dangerous manner. "You could have frightened Sam," she said.

Gary nodded toward Sam. "He's fine. I light the fire like this all the time when we go camping."

"And your mother lets you?"

A look of discomfort passed across Gary's face. "Well, she doesn't actually like it."

Martha would have said more, but Laura jumped up and down. "Where are the marshmallows?" she said. "Let's make some s'mores."

Gary went off to fetch the graham crackers and the marshmallows while Laura warmed her hands over the fire. Martha wondered why. The sun was still high in the sky but it was not too cold.

"There's always something comforting about a fire," Laura said, as if guessing her thoughts.

"You're going to show us how to play your card game, aren't you?" Sheryl asked her.

Martha smiled. "Yes, Dutch Blitz. I've brought my deck of cards." She missed playing the game with her *familye*. She wished her *schweschders* and Mary were with her now. She didn't have much in common with the *Englischers*. *But you're* Englisch *now*, she told herself.

"So what are the rules?" Gary asked her. "Do you play for money?"

Martha laughed.

"Of course the Amish don't play for money," Sheryl scolded him. "They probably think gambling is illegal. Is that right, Martha?"

Martha did not like answering so many questions. "We don't gamble," she said in a small voice.

It wasn't long before Gary was making s'mores for everyone. "We can't all make our own or Sam will want to make his own," he whispered to the women.

Martha kept a protective eye on Sam. She was concerned, as Gary didn't appear to be the most responsible person in the world. She noticed Gary wasn't watching Sam at all times and that worried her. Still, she thought she was probably being overprotective.

After that they all consumed several s'mores, Gary played the guitar and sang, and then Martha showed them all how to play Dutch Blitz. Sheryl and Laura caught on at once, but Gary kept complaining. "Can you explain the difference between the Blitz Pile, Post Piles, and Wood Pile again?" he asked continually.

After they played Dutch Blitz and then Scrabble, Sheryl and Gary decided to make dinner. Laura sat next to Martha and chatted. "Tell me all about your Amish friends," she said.

Martha was puzzled. "Well, I have a lot of friends," she said. "My sisters and Mary are my friends."

"And your sisters married Moses's brothers, didn't they?" Laura asked.

An uneasy feeling settled over Martha. "Yes, Hannah married Noah Hostetler, and Esther married Jacob Hostetler."

"How many brothers are there?"

"Only two unmarried ones," Martha said. "Moses and Elijah."

Laura narrowed her eyes. "Is Moses a good friend of yours?"

A heavy sinking feeling settled in Martha's stomach. "Yes, he's a good friend. I grew up with him," she said.

Laura nodded slowly. "That's nice." She bit her lip and stared at the fire before speaking once more. "What's he like?"

"Moses? He's nice, of course."

"He went with you to New York, didn't he?"

"Yes."

Laura turned to stare at her. "What was that like?"

Martha decided to mistake her meaning deliberately. "New York was much busier than anything I've ever experienced. I've never seen so many people in one place. It was good of course, because I got the contract for my chocolate business."

"Did you and Moses spend a lot of time together?"

Martha wished Sheryl would come back so Laura would stop asking her questions. "We went there on the train together."

"And you had dinner together?"

Martha nodded.

"Are you and Moses dating?"

Martha's hand flew to her throat. "No, of course not. Nothing like that."

Laura eyed her speculatively. "So you're just friends?"

"Yes, that's right." The whole conversation left

Martha entirely uncomfortable, but to her relief Sheryl and Gary did return at that moment.

"We've been talking about dinner," Gary said. "We're having canned soup and bagels, and the Dutch cabbage rolls Martha made. Oh, and baked beans. Or we could skip the main course and go directly to the three layer chocolate cake."

Martha didn't want to eat cake for dinner, so said, "Canned soup, bagels, and Dutch cabbage rolls sound good to me. What about the rest of you?"

They all agreed. Besides, Martha did not think Sam should eat cake for dinner. Martha fetched them plastic plates and forks and put them on the picnic table. Sam walked over and showed her a rock. "That's a lovely rock," she exclaimed.

"Let me see," Laura said. "That must be one of the nicest rocks I've ever seen. Well done, Sam."

Martha was pleased to see that Laura was good with him. Sam sat on the dirt next to the picnic table, but Laura patted the chair. "Why don't you sit with me and you can show me your rock again?"

Sam stood up and sat opposite Laura. Gary had told Martha previously that most children on the autism spectrum like their own space, so she figured that's why Sam had wanted to sit alone. She placed a plastic dish and spoon in front of Sam. "Would you like some lemonade, Sam?" she asked him. He nodded, so Martha went over to fetch the bottle.

Soon, they were all enjoying one of the strangest meals Martha had ever consumed, baked beans, soup, Dutch cabbage rolls, bagels, and three layer chocolate cake.

Gary told some jokes over dinner that were not at all funny, but everyone laughed no doubt to be polite. Gary laughed hardest of all.

"It's bedtime now, Sam," Gary said. Sam clutched the sticks and rocks and went into his tent with Gary. After five minutes, Gary returned. "Where are the other sticks we collected today?" Martha asked Gary.

"They're next to Sam's bed," Gary said. "Thanks for being so good with him, all of you."

"He's a great kid," Laura said. "My little cousin's on the autism spectrum."

Martha nodded to herself. That's why Laura was so understanding with Sam. She hoped she would not be left alone with Laura again, because Laura would no doubt take the opportunity to interrogate her about Moses. Martha certainly didn't want that.

Martha and Sheryl washed the plates while Gary and Laura dried them. "Now what will we do?" Laura said. "Will we play Scrabble again?"

"Anything but that Amish card game," Gary said with a chuckle. "Wait until I get the beer," Gary said. "Or wine?"

Sheryl and Laura both said they would have Chardonnay, but Martha declined. "I'll stick with lemonade," she said.

They sat near the fire and played Scrabble again. Martha considered this was quite comforting after all. It was just like being back home. Sam awoke and came out at intervals to check where Gary was.

After Martha went to bed, she drifted off several times while Sheryl and Laura were talking. The last thing she remembered before she fell asleep was Laura asking Sheryl how she could afford designer clothes and Sheryl was telling her they were knock-offs, whatever that meant. Martha made a mental note to ask Sheryl what knock-offs were.

Martha awoke suddenly in the night. She heard footsteps going past the tent. Maybe it was just Gary walking down to the bathroom facilities.

Still, the footsteps sounded very quiet. Martha had fallen asleep in her clothes, so she crawled to the tent flap to look out. There, in the small shafts of moonlight peeking through the clouds, was a small figure scurrying off into the trees. Sam!

Martha pulled on her boots. She shook Sheryl. "Get Gary! Sam's run off by himself."

Sheryl grunted and sat up while Martha ran out of the tent. She headed in the direction Sam was going, but couldn't find him. It was dark and the clouds were now hiding the moon once more.

Where was Sam? He had vanished into the night.

Chapter Fourteen

Martha hurried through the woods as fast as she dared in the dark. If only the clouds would drift away so the moon could illuminate her path.

"Sam!" she called out at the top of her lungs for the umpteenth time. There was no sign of him, but for all she knew he could be sitting quite close and she wouldn't see him.

Just then the moon peeked out from behind the clouds a little and Martha recognized her surroundings. It was the little track on the way to the fallen tree where Sam had found his unusual sticks. Maybe he was headed there now.

As she ran in the direction of the fallen tree, Martha was glad she was wearing jeans and not her Amish skirt. She had not gone far when she caught her foot in a tree root, falling heavily.

Martha rolled over and sat up gingerly, dusting herself down. A searing hot pain shot through her left foot. It was all Martha could do not to burst into tears with the pain and the shock. She clutched her ankle. It was already swelling in her walking boot, so she pulled off the boot and then yelped with pain.

Martha decided to leave the boot there. It was no help. She stood up and leaned against a tree, trying to steady her breathing. "Sam!" she called out again. Then she tried something else. "Sam, it's Martha. Can you help me? I'm hurt."

She waited a while, but there was no sign of Sam. At least the clouds had drifted away from the moon and Martha could clearly see. She doubted anyone would find her for some time. "All I can do is go to the fallen tree," Martha said aloud to herself. "I don't think it's much further."

Martha tried to step forward, but cried out with the pain. She leaned against the tree once more, and wondered what to do. Either she stayed there until dawn and waited for someone to find her, or she would somehow try to make it to the fallen tree. Martha figured she had not fallen enough to break her ankle, but she had broken both ankles in the buggy accident and that left her quite concerned. Martha sent up a silent prayer to *Gott* that He would keep her safe and lead her to Sam.

Martha spotted a branch lying on the ground so picked it up. She figured if she could lean on it, she could hobble her way toward the fallen tree. She gingerly took one little step and then breathed a sigh of relief. So far so good. She didn't think her ankle was badly injured after all, but it sure hurt.

Martha edged forward ever so slowly, stopping

every few moments to rest. At one point she felt she couldn't go on, so she stopped and gulped the fresh night air. She could hear something in the bushes. "Sam, is that you?" she called out.

Whatever it was moved away from her fast, faster than a child. *Maybe it was a deer*, Martha thought.

After a few moments, Martha rallied herself. "You have to find that child," she said aloud. "You can do it!" With that, she hobbled on some more.

Martha had no idea how long she had been walking, until the clearing came into sight. There, sitting on the ground was Sam, twirling a stick between his fingers.

"Sam!" Martha cried with relief. She hurried over to him as fast she could, which was not fast at all, given the pain in her ankle and the fact she could not put her full weight on it.

Sam did not react to her presence. She knew not to hug him, because he liked to have his own personal space. Martha gently lowered herself onto the ground and sat next to him. Sam showed Martha a stick. It was an unusual stick with lots of knots.

"What a lovely stick," Martha said. "Sam, we have to get back to Gary. Gary will be worried about you."

Sam simply showed Martha another stick by way of response.

"That's a lovely stick too," Martha said. "Sam, I've hurt my ankle. Do you think you can help me get back to the campsite?"

Sam did not look at her but kept twirling the stick. Martha ran a hand across her brow. What was she to do? It would take her an age to get back to the campsite, but they couldn't sit here all night. The others would be worried and looking for them by now. And what if she was making her way back and Sam ran away from her? She would never find him then, and that could be quite dangerous for him.

Martha sat there for some time pondering what to do while Sam continued to twirl the stick. A large crack of thunder sounded overhead, and the first drops of rain fell. Martha took off her coat and put it around Sam's shoulders. He did not seem to object. Martha did not want to stay out there for hours with the two of them being drenched. There was no shelter in sight. There was nothing else for it—she would have to go back to the campground.

Suddenly, Martha had an idea. "Let's go back to Gary, but let's look for interesting sticks and stones on the way," she said. "Do you think that's a good idea, Sam?"

With that, he stood up. Martha breathed a big sigh of relief. If Sam thought they were looking for sticks, then surely he would not run away from her.

Sam hurried down the track, but Martha called after him. "Wait for me. Sam. I've hurt my foot and I'll have to go slowly."

Sam stopped and waited, but continued looking down the track. It took Martha a while to struggle to her feet. She pulled herself up on the fallen log and seized the long stick.

She hobbled after Sam as fast as she could, but

it seemed that every time she had almost caught up with him, he would hurry forward.

Martha thought she should do something to attract his attention. Fortunately, she saw an unusual stick in a Y-shape. "Sam, look at this stick," she said.

Sam turned around and ran back. He picked up the stick and looked at it this way and that and then tucked it under his arm.

That was how they progressed for the next hour, Sam getting too far ahead of her, and then Martha finding a stick or a rock on the path to show him. Sam didn't seem happy with most of the sticks or stones that she found, tossing them aside after he inspected them, but at least he stayed with her.

The going was slow and Martha continually had to lean against a tree to rest. Each time, she asked Sam to show her the sticks. Although she repeated this umpteen times, Sam did not appear to mind showing her the same sticks over and over again.

Martha was worried, wondering what was going on back at camp. Surely they were all looking for them. They must be awfully concerned. There were so many tracks through the woods and no one knew which one she had taken. She had already passed her boot and no one had found that. She left her boot there, because she wasn't able to carry it anyway.

The pain in her ankle was getting worse and Martha fought bouts of nausea, which hit her again and again. Sometimes, stabbing pains as sharp as a knife pierced her foot.

The rain fell harder, so Martha called Sam over.

She wrapped the coat tightly around him. "Try to keep dry," she said.

Sam clutched the coat to him with one hand and clutched the stick with his other hand. "Okay," he said. "Is it much further?"

"I don't know how far it is," Martha said truthfully. "I can't go fast because I've hurt my foot."

"Okay," Sam said again.

Martha wished she had taken a flashlight with her. It was foolish of her not to take one, but then again she had been in such a hurry to catch Sam that she hadn't even looked for one in the tent. If she had a flashlight, she could shine it on the treetops and maybe someone would see it. Still, there was no point wishing she had done so, because she hadn't. She would just have to make the most of it.

It seemed like an age before Martha came out onto the main track. Within moments, she heard someone calling. "We're here!" she called back at the top of her lungs. When there was no response, she called again "We're here! It's me, Martha, and I've got Sam." This time she called so loudly that her throat hurt.

Soon she heard footsteps. Gary burst into view. "Sam!" he said. He ran over to Sam and hugged him. Sam didn't pull away, but he stood there stiffly, his arms by his sides. Gary released him. "Martha, you're hurt."

Now that everything was all right, Martha crumbled onto the ground clutching her ankle. She was unable to stop the tears that sprang to her eyes. Gary ran over and put his arm around her shoulders. "I'll go and get help," he said. "Wait here."

"Martha." The voice was familiar.

She looked up and saw Moses. Was she dreaming? "What are you doing here?" she said. She was aware the words came out like an accusation.

"Martha, you're hurt," Moses said too.

Gary at once took his arm away from around Martha's shoulders. Martha felt guilty, but she had nothing to feel guilty about.

Martha hurried to explain. "I woke up when I heard footsteps outside the tent, and I looked out to see Sam running into the woods. I called to everyone and ran after him, but then I hurt my foot. I guessed he was going to the fallen tree with the unusual sticks, and that's where I found him, but I hurt my foot on the way. That's why we took so long coming back."

Gary was clutching Sam's hand tightly. "Thank you, Martha. Thank you so much." Martha thought Gary looked on the point of tears. In fact, he wiped his eyes. "I was just about to call Mom and tell her. Thank goodness I don't have to worry her. Sam's all right."

Martha was doing her best not to burst into tears. "Moses, how did you know what happened? Did somebody call you?"

"Yes, Sheryl called the barn. My father was working late and took the call." Moses hesitated, and then added, "I gave Sheryl our number at dinner the other night and asked her to call me if you ever needed help."

"Moses was just about to call K-9 Search and Rescue, the fire company, and a police helicopter," Gary said with a forced laugh. "He was beside himself."

Martha looked up, wondering if he was joking.

"We were so worried. *I* was so worried about you," Moses said. He put his arm around Martha and helped her to her feet.

Martha looked around her. "I lost my stick I was leaning on," she said as she all but fell into Moses.

Moses scooped her up in her arms as if she was as light as feather and carried her back to the camping area. Martha was embarrassed that Moses was carrying her, but she was glad of his strength and his warmth. She had no idea he was so strong. When he reached the camp, Laura and Sheryl hurried over. "What happened?" they said in unison.

"Martha has hurt her ankle and she's broken it before," Moses said, concern evident in his voice. He gently deposited Martha onto a camp chair. "Do you have any ice?"

Soon Moses was holding an ice pack on Martha's ankle. "Does that help?" he asked her.

She smiled weakly. "*Jah*. It's better now that I'm not having to walk on it." Moses was here and he was looking after her. It made her all warm and fuzzy inside.

"Where is your first aid kit?" Moses asked Gary.

His request was met with a blank look. "I don't have one," Gary said.

"I always carry a bandage in my purse," Sheryl said.

Laura's jaw fell open. "You do? Why?"

"Because I sprained my wrist once and it was terribly painful. I did it by falling down the stairs, and a bandage brought me great relief, so I've carried a bandage ever since in my purse. It's kind of a superstition."

Martha thought it a strange thing to say, and clearly so did Laura, but Martha was simply glad for the bandage. Moses gently bandaged her ankle. She wondered how someone who was so strong could be so gentle.

While Moses was bandaging Martha's ankle, he called out, "Martha needs to have her foot elevated. Do you have anything like a cooler?"

Sheryl hurried forward with a cooler.

"Where's Gary? Is Sam all right?" Martha asked.

Moses shot her a sharp look when she asked where Gary was, but Martha simply wanted to know if he was tending to Sam. She thought she had better explain. "Sam was soaking wet and I'm hoping Gary is getting him a change of dry clothes," she said.

Sheryl hurried to reassure her. "Yes, I'm sure that's what they're doing now. I know Gary can be a bit silly at times, but he does look after Sam."

Not enough not to let Sam out of his tent at night, Martha thought, and then realized she was being unkind. After all, he could hardly lock the tent door, and it wasn't his fault he didn't wake up when Sam left the tent.

"I'll have to take you to have that ankle seen to now," Moses said.

Martha made to protest, but Moses crossed his arms over his chest. "Martha, you had a serious injury to that ankle and you can't take any chances. I won't take no for an answer."

"*Denki*." Martha was secretly cut happy that Moses had taken charge. "My ankle *is* feeling better now I'm not walking on it," she added.

"I'll drive you," Laura volunteered. "That is, if Gary doesn't mind if I take his car?"

Gary had come out of the tent. Martha noticed his face was white and drawn. He was clutching his chest. "I've got Sam into dry clothes and dried his hair. He's fallen fast asleep. He's none the worse for wear, thank goodness. In fact, he seems pleased about his adventure. I'm not going to go back to sleep tonight though, in case he tries it again. This was a terrible idea, taking him camping."

"Has he ever wandered off like that before?" Sheryl asked him.

"Of course not, or I wouldn't have brought him." Gary sounded somewhat offended. "It's probably because Mom isn't here."

"We're taking Martha to the doctor. Can I borrow your car?" Laura asked him.

"Of course. I'll just fetch the keys." Gary hurried to the tent and came back, tossing the keys to Laura. "Thank you so much, Martha. I don't know what I would have done without you. Thank you so much."

"You're welcome," Martha said, wincing as Moses

helped her to her feet. This time Moses did not carry her, but helped her over to the car.

"What's the address of your doctor?" Laura asked him. "I'll put it in my GPS. But surely, a doctor won't see Martha at this time of night? It's after hours. He'll be shut."

Moses shook his head. "No, we'll go to Mrs. Graber's. She'll see us. She sees people in our community after hours for emergencies at her house."

"Wow! That's amazing." Laura seemed quite shocked. "Should you call her and warn her that you're on the way?"

"She doesn't have phone in her house," Moses said. "We'll have to go there. It's either that or take Martha to the hospital."

"Please don't take me to the hospital," Martha pleaded.

Moses gave Laura Mrs. Graber's address. It seemed they were there in no time at all.

Laura stayed in the car with Martha while Moses went to knock. To Martha's relief, Mrs. Graber answered the door quickly.

Moses hurried back to help Martha out of the car.

"Thank you for seeing us so late at in the middle of the night," Moses said to Mrs. Graber.

Mrs. Graber shot them a warm smile. "I just had someone here for stomach ache," she said. "Sit Martha on the couch, if you would, and then go and make us all some chamomile-and-ginger tea."

Laura looked at Moses. "Do you know how to make it?"

"*Jah*, I'll show you." The two of them walked toward the kitchen, leaving Martha to wonder why Moses and Laura both needed to make meadow tea. Surely Moses hadn't needed to invite Laura along.

Mrs. Graber peered at Martha's foot. "Moses put ice on it and bandaged it," Martha told her.

Mrs. Graber nodded as she removed the bandage. "*En Schtich in Zeit is neine wart schpaeder naus.*" *A stitch in time saves nine.*

Martha told her about Sam running away when she was camping, and added, "And then I didn't see tree roots on the ground and I tripped heavily. The trouble is, I had to walk on it a long way after that."

"It's swollen, but I don't think it's broken," Mrs. Graber said. "You should see the *doktor* in the morning and have it x-rayed. I also don't think it's a bad sprain. If you had been able to stop when you first did it, I'm sure it would have been a lot better. Has the pain worsened?"

"Walking on the pain is nowhere near as bad as it was before Moses put the ice on it and bandaged it. It seems a lot better now," Martha said. "If I keep it perfectly still, I can't feel it at all. It's only if it moves a bit in a certain direction."

Mrs. Graber rubbed salve into the foot. "This is arnica," she said. "I will bandage it again after you drink some chamomile-and-ginger tea which will help with the pain. Keep it elevated as much as you can. Come and see me again after you receive the x-ray results if you have any concerns. I wouldn't worry, if I were you. The thing is, you need to rest it and avoid walking on it."

"But I'm on *rumspringa* and I work in a café every morning," Martha protested.

Mrs. Graber shook her head. "You need to stay off this foot for a week," she said.

Martha was disappointed. She was even more disappointed when Moses and Laura returned with the tea. The two were laughing, their heads close together.

Chapter Fifteen

The following morning, Martha thought of her ankle immediately upon awakening. She moved it a little and was pleased to note it had improved overnight. Mrs. Graber's remedies certainly worked. She got out of bed and tested it gingerly. The foot took her weight, but it hurt to walk on it. She hopped into the kitchen and made some coffee. It was hard to get from the kitchen to the couch while hopping with a full cup of coffee, so Martha hobbled. The pain had gone, but her ankle felt weak.

Martha sat and sipped her coffee slowly. Gary had insisted on driving her to the doctor that day. Moses had looked quite put out after they had arrived back from Mrs. Graber's the previous night, and it was only after Moses left that Gary told Martha he felt responsible. He insisted it was his fault that she had a sore ankle, because it was his fault that Sam had run away. Martha had tried to reassure him, but he would have none of it. He was clearly guilt-ridden.

Sam, however, was none the worse for wear, Gary had reported. He had taken it in his stride and seemed particularly pleased with the new collection of sticks he had gathered in the dark.

Martha wondered if Moses thought perhaps there was something between herself and Gary. She knew Moses well and she wouldn't have been surprised if that's what he was thinking. Gary hadn't explained to him explicitly that he felt it was all his fault, and Moses might have misinterpreted Gary's insistence on driving Martha to the doctor.

Gary and Sam stayed in the waiting room while the doctor poked and prodded Martha's ankle. "I'm going to send you for an x-ray, Martha," the doctor said. "I'm fairly certain it isn't broken, but I don't want to take any chances, especially since you broke both your ankles in the buggy accident. We can't be too careful, you know."

Martha saw the wisdom of the doctor's words, but she didn't want to go back to the hospital. After all, she and her sisters had spent some time there after the buggy accident.

And so, an hour later, Martha was waiting in a cold, clinical waiting room waiting to be taken into X-Ray. The staff were kindly and put her at ease, but she was nervous. She had called the café and told them the doctor had sent her for an x-ray. They had seemed concerned and told her not to worry, but she *did* worry. She had a job and she felt responsible. Still, what choice did she have?

Finally, Martha was summoned. She went through

a door, only to be told to sit on a seat inside the door. Martha had thought she would be going straight to have the x-ray, but instead she was told she had to sit on the seat. She was there a considerable time, and saw other people coming and going. She wondered why they hadn't left her in the main waiting room. Finally, an orderly came along and asked her if she needed a wheelchair. "I don't think so," Martha said and made to hobble forward, but the orderly waved her back to her chair.

"You definitely need a wheelchair," he said. "You shouldn't be walking on that foot. Not until we know what's wrong with it."

He ducked into another room and before long returned with a wheelchair. He pushed Martha down a long corridor and around a corner into the x-ray room. Martha was distraught at being back in a wheelchair again. She had spent so long in one and it was all happening again. *You're overreacting*, she silently scolded herself. *Mrs. Graber and the doctor don't even think it's broken.* She wanted to ask the x-ray technician if her ankle was broken, but she didn't think he would tell her.

The technician took an x-ray and then left the room. Moments later, he popped his head back around the door and said, "I'm new at this and the doctor wants several x-rays. I'll be back in a moment."

He returned with a short woman with a shock of white hair. "Yes, the doctor *does* want a lot of x-rays," she said, scratching her chin. She made Martha lie this way and that while they took plenty of x-rays.

"Are you allowed to tell me if my ankle's broken?" Martha asked the woman, who was clearly the technician's senior.

"I wouldn't worry if I were you," she said with a wink. "Who's the doctor again?" She looked at her notes. "I see. You have to take the x-rays back to the doctor in person. Just go back to reception and we'll send them through when we're ready. We won't keep you waiting long."

Martha thanked her, and the x-ray technician pushed her back to the waiting room in a wheelchair. Gary was wringing his hands nervously. "Broken?" he asked anxiously.

"I don't think so," Martha said. "I'm pretty sure they hinted that it wasn't."

Gary breathed a long sigh of relief. "I'm so relieved," he said. "Where do we go now?"

"We have to wait until they print the x-rays or something," Martha said. "They shouldn't be long."

After about five minutes, the lady summoned Martha over. She made to get out of the wheelchair, but the lady waved her back down. "Your young man there can push you to your car," she called out, "and then he can bring the wheelchair back here."

"Sure," Gary said. He pushed Martha over to the reception desk, and the lady handed Martha a large gray envelope.

Martha was a little awkward that the lady had called Gary her young man, but she was hardly going to correct her. After all, they were strangers and they wouldn't care one way or another.

"I can't thank you enough," Gary said.

Martha waved one hand at him. "You're welcome, but please don't worry, Gary. Anyone would have done what I did. The main thing is that Sam is safe."

"I was sick with worry over him last night," Gary said. "It was silly of me to take him camping. It's just that I thought he would be so disappointed if we didn't go."

"Everything is easy in hindsight," Martha said, doing her best to make him feel better.

Martha didn't have long to wait when she was back at her own doctor's. Five minutes after she handed the receptionist her x-rays, the doctor called her in. "Good news, Martha. It's not broken and the original break looks very good indeed. I'm quite pleased with it," he said by way of greeting.

"Then what's wrong with my ankle?" she asked him.

"It's a bit of a sprain with considerable bruising," he said. "I don't think it's serious at all. Just keep it elevated and bandaged. The main thing is to keep off it. I don't think it would have been such a problem if you hadn't walked on it so far. Do you need something for the pain?"

Martha shook her head. "It doesn't really hurt. It's just a dull ache that doesn't go away. It's a bit irritating, but it's not as if it hurts."

"If it does start to hurt or if it gets any worse, let me know. The main thing is to stay off it."

"I've been working at a café every morning for

five days a week," Martha told him. "How long before I can go back?"

The doctor scratched his chin. "Given your history with that leg, I'd prefer it if you stayed off your feet all week."

"Not again," Martha lamented. The doctor shot her a look, so she added, "I had all those weeks of lying around the house not doing anything. I'm not used to being idle and I was awfully bored. Now I'll have to go back to being bored again."

The doctor scratched his chin once more. "But you're on *rumspringa* now, aren't you?"

Martin nodded.

"Well, surely you have internet and TV."

Martha realized the kindly doctor wouldn't understand, so she simply smiled and nodded. "Are you sure I can't go back to work any sooner?" she asked him.

"I would think it's best to be on the safe side, given your history, that you rest up all week and keep that leg elevated."

"But didn't you say you were pleased with the way my leg has healed after the buggy accident?" Martha asked him.

"Yes, I'm quite pleased with it. The thing is, I don't want to put any strain on your other leg."

"But my other leg is fine," Martha said.

"It's now the supporting leg. A supporting leg can develop problems if it has to take the weight and do all the work for the injured leg. It's not such a hardship, is it, just one week resting up?"

"I suppose not," Martha said with a sigh. The doctor smiled and showed her to the door.

"Is something wrong?" Gary asked. "You look really upset."

"It's just that I have to sit around all week doing nothing," Martha lamented. "The doctor gave me a certificate to show them at work."

"Lucky thing." Gary patted her on her back as he helped her outside. "A free holiday."

"But I won't get paid," Martha said. "I'm only casual."

Gary's face fell. "Never mind, you can watch Netflix. I know! You can work on your chocolate business."

Martha nodded slowly. "Gary, that's a great idea. I can make plans all week." Martha spirits were lifted. She turned to Gary and laughed. "That's fantastic, Gary. Why didn't I think of that?"

Gary had his arm under her elbow, helping her to his car. Just then Martha looked up and saw Moses. She had not even noticed him standing there. *Why does it always happen like this?* Martha asked herself. *I'm sure Moses must think something is going on between me and Gary. I'm sure he thinks we must be dating.*

She wanted to say something to Moses, but then again, she and Moses could never be together. She was going to stay *Englisch* and not return to the Amish.

"How is your leg?" Moses asked her.

"It's not broken. I had heaps of x-rays this morning," Martha told him, "and the original injury has healed up very nicely. The doctor said he was pleased the way it's healed."

"*Wunderbar*!" Moses said.

"But the bad thing is I have to rest up all week and I'm not allowed to go to work," Martha said.

"I let your parents know what happened to you, and your *vadder* wants you to call him and tell him the results. Is it a serious sprain?"

Martha shook her head. "*Nee*, the *doktor* said it's only a slight sprain, but he doesn't want me to put any more stress on my body by having to carry myself differently. At least I think that's what he said. Anyway, he insisted I rest up. I have to keep my foot elevated and not use it. I was upset about it, but Gary just suggested I could work on my chocolate business."

The two men exchanged glances.

"I'm just driving her back to her apartment now," Gary said. "See you later, Moses."

Martha had wanted to speak with Moses some more, but Gary had his hand under her arm and was guiding her to his car. Martha was a little upset at Gary's blunt dismissal of Moses, but what could she do?

She looked back over her shoulder at Moses. He did not look at all pleased.

Chapter Sixteen

When Martha got home, Gary helped her into her apartment and left her on the couch with her foot up on the coffee table. As soon as Gary was out the door, Martha realized she didn't have any paper to make notes about her chocolate business. She wished she had thought of that before Gary left. She was about to get up and look for some when she remembered she had to call her father at his work and tell him how her ankle was.

"Martha!" her father exclaimed. "How is your foot?"

"It's *gut*, *denki*, and the *doktor* said he is happy with how my old injuries have healed. However, he said I had to take the week off work."

"That's wise," her father said. "Mary asked me to give you a message."

Martha was mystified. "What is it?"

"Mary mentioned a boy called Sam. She said she promised to show him the dog, Pirate. She wondered if you could come home and the two of you could go and visit the dog with the little boy."

"Well, I'll ask Gary if Sam can visit," Martha said. "Their mother is ill. Their parents divorced some time ago and I don't know where their father is. Did Mary tell you that Sam is on the autism spectrum?"

"*Jah*," Mr. Miller said. "Can you come home and visit, Martha?"

"Sure," Martha said. She hung up, just as there was a knock at the door. Martha struggled to stand up, and hobbled over to open the door.

"I forgot I hadn't left you any food or anything," Gary said. "I'm sorry. I'm not good at looking after people."

"It would be good if you could make me some coffee, please, and fetch me some food. And also, I have a bunch of notes on my nightstand. There's a pen there as well. Would you bring them out to me please?"

Gary hurried off to do as she asked. When he returned, she said, "I was just speaking to my father on the phone…"

Gary interrupted her. "I thought you weren't allowed to have phones?"

"My father makes furniture and he has a phone at his business. We are allowed to have phones at our workplaces and even computers."

Gary gasped. "Computers!" he said in horror.

Martha could not help but laugh at the expression on his face. "Anyways, my father said Mary had promised to show Sam her dog. She wondered if you could take Sam to my parents' house and she can take him on a buggy ride to see the dog. I'll go too."

"When?" Gary said, looking at his watch.

"Well, any time that suits you, I suppose," Mary said.

"Do you need any notice?"

Martha pulled a face. "No, I don't think so."

Gary looked at his watch again. "Actually, this could get me out of quite a pickle. What if I drove you and Sam over to your parents' house now and then collected him just before dinner time tonight?"

Martha thought about it for a moment. "Sure. I suppose that's fine. I was only going to be sitting around here anyway, and I do miss my *familye*."

"That's great! I wanted to run a few errands, but I couldn't really do it with Sam. This will give me a chance get a lot done today. Do you want to leave now? How long will it take you to get ready?"

"I'm ready now," Martha said. "We can go immediately." Just then, she realized she wanted to wear her Amish clothes to visit her Amish parents. She knew most people on *rumspringa* didn't do that, but her mother was a little upset by her being on *rumspringa*, and she thought it would make her mother happier. "I had better change first."

Gary groaned. "You women always take hours to put on your make-up."

Martha chuckled. "I'm not putting on any make-up." She hurried to her bedroom and changed her clothes quickly. She remembered when she had a broken arm, and changing clothes took forever and was painful. However, changing clothes with a sore ankle was quite easy.

When she walked back out, Gary gasped. "I'll never get used to seeing you in your national dress."

Martha chuckled. "National dress?" She laughed again.

Gary flushed beet red. "Whatever you call it. Anyway, I'll pop back to my apartment and get Sam."

Sam showed no reaction to Martha dressed in her Amish dress, cape, apron, prayer *kapp*, and bonnet. He simply showed her his collection of sticks, and once again Martha admired them. He showed her a particular rock.

"I've never seen a rock like this before," Martha said. "It's beautiful and shiny."

"It's black tourmaline," Gary said. "Sam saw it in a shop and pointed to it, so I just had to get it for him."

Sam turned the stone over and over again before resuming twirling one of his sticks.

Martha directed Gary to her house. When he brought the car to a stop just outside the house, he said, "Wow, this is not far at all. I had no idea you lived so close."

"It's not that close in a buggy," Martha said.

"Look, Martha, this is really good of you to take Sam for the day, especially with your sore foot."

"There are plenty of people to look after him," Martha said.

Mary was in the garden and she hurried over, waving. "This is a nice surprise."

"I hope it's okay. Martha said it would be okay," Gary said anxiously. "Sam wants to see Pirate."

"Sure he can," Mary said. "He's over at a friend's house. We'll take him in the buggy."

"I think Sam would enjoy that," Gary said. "He loves animals. He loves horses too."

Laura had told Martha that children on the autism spectrum often relate to horses, and that there were in fact several charities specifically for children on the autism spectrum to interact with horses. Sam was busy showing Mary his black tourmaline, and she was exclaiming over it.

"Gary, would you like to come inside for some lemonade?" Martha asked.

"Err, no, um, no thanks," Gary stammered. Martha wondered if he was a little afraid of Amish people and afraid to meet her parents. "I'd better go. I'll call for you. I'll come back at exactly five?"

"Sure," Martha said. "Just text me if you change your plans."

"Sure." Gary waved, said goodbye to Sam, and drove off.

Martha watched them carefully to see if Sam was upset that Gary had driven away, but he didn't seem to mind at all. He hadn't even looked up and was still showing Mary his black tourmaline.

"I found a nice stone for you the other day," Mary said. "Would you like to come with me and get it?"

Sam said, "Yes," and followed Mary inside the house. Martha followed her and Rebecca ran out.

"Martha!" she exclaimed. "I didn't know you were coming. I'll go and tell *Mamm*."

Rebecca vanished and Martha was only just in the door when Mrs. Miller hurried out. She was smiling from ear to ear. "Martha. This is a surprise. This must be Sam." Sam did not look at Mrs. Miller, who continued, "Mary found a stone for you."

"Yes," Sam said again, but he did not look at Mrs. Miller. However, he smiled.

"You can have some lemonade while I fetch it," Mary said. "You sit right there and I'll come straight back."

Mrs. Miller handed Sam a glass of lemonade. He drank half of it and then put it on the coffee table in front of him. It wasn't long before Mary was back. She handed Sam a sizeable stone.

Sam stared at the stone with deep concentration, and then hugged it to him.

"I think he likes it," Mrs. Miller said. She kept smiling at Sam. Martha wondered if Mrs. Miller had ever wanted a son. She had four daughters, after all. Hannah had a twin girl and a twin boy. Mr. Miller always jokingly said he and Hannah's *sohn*, Mason, were outnumbered by women. Martha wondered if Esther would have a boy.

"Martha!"

Martha looked up and realized her mother had been speaking to her. "What is it, *Mamm*?"

"Are you back for good?"

"*Nee, Mamm*. I'm leaving at five this afternoon."

Mrs. Miller narrowed her eyes. "I see." Her tone was

icy. "I thought your father told me you had to rest for a week. I thought you would come home for the week."

"I have work to do," Martha said.

"Surely not on your bad foot," her mother snapped.

"*Nee, Mamm*," Martha said again. "I mean work on my chocolate business."

Mrs. Miller folded her arms over her chest. "I will go make some meadow tea," she snapped.

"Will you be able to come and see Pirate or will you have to stay here because of your foot?" Mary asked Martha.

"I'd rather come," Martha said. Silently, she added, *I think I'd better get away from* Mamm. *She's not in the best of moods.*

"Maybe you could sit inside with Mrs. Yoder, or maybe sit on the porch steps."

"The porch steps might be a good idea," Martha said and then laughed. "David won't mind us coming, will he?" She nodded her head slightly toward Sam.

Mary shook her head. "*Nee*, I told him that I would bring Sam to see Pirate."

After Martha and Mary drank the meadow tea and Sam had another glass of lemonade, Mary went to harness the horse. After five minutes or so, she stuck her head around the door and called out. "Come on, ready to go."

Martha hobbled a few steps and then Mary ran in and took her by the elbow. "I'm sorry, Martha, I forgot about your foot. Would you like to meet a horse, Sam?"

"Yes," Sam said.

"You go on ahead, Mary. I can walk on it pretty well now, because it's bandaged tightly," Martha said. She knew she wasn't supposed to walk on it at all, but she didn't think a short way would hurt. After all, she would have to walk about a little in the apartment.

By the time Martha made her way outside, Sam was hugging the horse. He had reached up, and had his arms around the horse's neck. The horse didn't seem to mind at all. In fact, he seemed to be enjoying the attention.

"Sam really does love animals," Mary said appreciatively. "Come on, Sam, do you want a buggy ride right now in this buggy?"

"Yes," Sam said.

Martha noted he was speaking more regularly than usual. Mary helped him up onto the buggy and then helped Martha up too. Martha kept a close eye on Sam to see if he was afraid of the buggy, but he seemed excited. He had even stopped twirling his stick and was looking around at the scenery. When they were a short way from the Yoders' farm, Mary said to Martha, "I hope Pirate's on his best behavior. I hope he doesn't jump up."

"I thought David trained him not to," Martha said.

"Yes, but I can't help worrying," Mary said. "He could easily knock Sam over."

There was no sign of Pirate or anyone else when Mary stopped the buggy outside the Yoders' house, but soon David walked around the side of the barn. "*Hullo*, Mary," he said with delight, followed by, "*Hiya*, Martha." He looked at Sam and smiled at him. "You must be Sam. Mary's told me about you."

Sam stared at his feet, twirling one of his sticks.

"I hope Pirate won't jump up and knock him down," Mary said.

"I'll keep a close eye on him, but he's been really good lately," David said.

Pirate bounded around the edge of the barn, obviously happy to see Mary. She flung her arms around his neck and kissed him. When she stood up, Sam flung his arms around Pirate's neck, and kissed his head too. Pirate gave him a long lick up the face and Sam giggled.

Martha was shocked. "That's the most excited I've seen Sam and I've spent a bit of time with him lately," she said.

Sam sat in the dust, and Pirate rolled over to have his belly rubbed. Sam chuckled with delight.

"Oh, sorry, Martha, I'll help you from the buggy," Mary said. To David, she said, "Martha twisted her ankle."

"Sorry to hear that," David said. "Here, I'll help you out of the buggy." When David and Martha reached the porch, David asked her, "Would you like to sit here on the porch?"

"*Jah, denki*," she said.

Martha sat there hoping Mrs. Yoder wouldn't come out and speak with her. She looked back over and saw Mary and Sam both tickling Pirate's tummy. "So Sam is the brother of a friend of Mary's?" David asked her.

Martha could see David looked none too pleased. His arms were folded over his chest and his expression was grim. She did not know how to respond. She did not know if Mary was trying to make him jealous and she didn't want to put her foot in it. "*Jah*," she said. "Sam is Gary's little brother."

"And who is this Gary?" David was still frowning.

"He lives in my apartment building," Martha said. "He's a friend of my roommate, Sheryl."

"Are Sheryl and Gary dating?" David asked her.

Martha chuckled. "No, of course not. No, they're just friends."

David pursed his lips. "So how did Mary meet this Gary?"

Martha suppressed a smile. *So David is jealous, after all*, she thought. Hannah had told her that David had been running around with *Englisch* girls, but that was some time ago now. Maybe David had come to his senses. She hadn't heard any rumors about him for quite some time. Maybe he had, in fact, gotten over his youthful ways and was ready to settle down.

"Mary came to my apartment recently and Gary was there," she said. "Mary told them about Pirate and thought Sam would like to see him."

"And so Gary isn't married or dating anyone?" David asked her.

"No, he isn't." Martha tried not to smile too much.

Martha was excited. She knew Mary had told her she liked David, and it seemed that David liked Mary. The more she thought about it, the more obvious it was to her. Yet why hadn't David and Mary made their feelings known to each other? Martha thought it a little strange. Maybe they were both too shy.

Chapter Seventeen

A week later, Martha returned from work tired and frustrated. Laura had been talking about Moses continually, and had hinted more than once that Martha should invite them both over for dinner again.

As soon as she walked inside the apartment, there was a loud knock on the door. Martha turned around and opened the door to see two police officers on the doorstep. One handed her papers, which he called a *warrant*, and the other informed her that she had to accompany them to the police station. Martha saw that her name was on the warrant, and so was Sheryl's.

"Why, what, why?" she stammered. She was so shocked that she didn't quite understand what the officers were telling her. One photographed her and then walked around taking photographs of the apartment.

Martha realized that one of the officers was speaking to her. "Sorry, what did you say?"

"That purse you are carrying is a stolen Gucci."

"It can't be," Martha said. "Sheryl let me borrow

it." The officer simply made a speech to Martha, the only words of which she understood in her confusion were *arrest, felony, right to remain silent*. The officer then put handcuffs on her and led her away.

Martha sat in the interview room at the police station. She was in shock and unable to take in what the officers were saying to her. They made her repeat the same thing over and over again, and then some.

"So your story is that you are an Amish girl on *rumspringa*. You answered a newspaper advertisement and are renting a room from Sheryl Garner in her apartment. You have been working as a short order cook. You have no non-Amish clothes, so Sheryl Garner has been letting you borrow hers. You allege that you borrowed them at her suggestion."

"Yes," Martha said yet again, trying hard to bite back tears.

"And you allege that you had no knowledge of Sheryl's activities."

Martha did burst into tears this time. "No," she said between sobs.

"This is your first offense," one of the officers said. "If you tell us all you know, it will be better for you. You'll get a lighter sentence. It will be a misdemeanor of the first degree. Otherwise, you could be facing charges of felony of the third degree. The penalty for that is seven years in jail, or a fine of between $2,500 and $15,000, or maybe both jail *and* a fine."

"But I don't know anything," Martha said, dabbing at her eyes with a tissue, and shifting uncomfortably on the hard, green, plastic chair. Her legs had gone to sleep as she had been sitting there for so long. She could see that the officers didn't believe her. What a nightmare this was! What had Sheryl done? Perhaps she should not have refused her right to a criminal defense lawyer. She had no idea where she'd get one anyway. Martha was confused and frightened. The fingerprinting and the photographs had been humiliating. She had been treated like a criminal. In fact, the officers clearly thought she *was* a criminal. What would happen now?

"If you can't afford an attorney," one of the officers continued, "you are entitled to an attorney paid for and appointed by the state. This means you don't have to pay for the attorney," he said slowly to Martha, in case she hadn't understood.

"But I've done nothing wrong," Martha said. "I don't need an attorney."

Just then there was a loud commotion and both officers hurried outside. One returned soon after and said, "There's been an incident. We have to clear the area. Do you have any objection if we place you in a holding cell for a short time until we can recommence questioning?"

"I suppose that's okay," Martha said, still unsure of her rights and the ramifications of whatever she happened to agree to. This was all completely foreign to her.

The officer hurriedly led her down several corridors, until they reached an area into which they were buzzed by a uniformed police officer. Martha gasped when they walked through. In front of her stretched rows and rows of cold, steel bars and cold, concrete floors. Much to her dismay, Martha was put into one of the holding cells with another woman. Martha eyed the woman apprehensively. She looked young, and not at all like Martha imagined a criminal to look, but then again, Martha had never imagined Sheryl as a criminal either. Martha took in the girl's long, blonde hair, her vivid blue eyes, and her pale skin.

Martha tentatively took a seat on the bench, as far away from the girl as possible. For a moment neither spoke, and then the girl asked shyly, "What are you in for?"

Martha looked at the girl. She didn't look dangerous, but Martha was wary. "My roommate's been stealing clothes, and the police think I'm involved in it, too."

"And are you?"

Martha shook her head. "No. What about you?"

"I fell in with a bad crowd. They stole a car, and I was riding in it. We were all arrested, but I didn't know it was stolen. I'm Amish. I'm on my *rumspringa*." The girl shivered.

"But I'm on my *rumspringa* too!" Martha exclaimed.

The girl's whole demeanor changed. "You are? That's *wunderbar*!" she gushed. "I'm Sarah Beachy. I'm from Kentucky, not from around here. I don't know any Amish here. I've left the Amish forever."

"Me too," said Martha, surprised at Sarah's words, but then amended it to, "At least, I'm considering it.

My name's Martha Miller." It was clear to her that *Gott* had caused the two of them to meet. This surely could not be a coincidence.

"I'm all by myself," Sarah said, and then burst into hysterical sobs.

Martha was at a loss. She simply patted the girl on the back and made soothing noises.

"Sorry about that," Sarah managed to say. "My *mudder* passed away and my *daed* remarried, and his new *fraa* doesn't like me, so I left."

"What about your *bruders* and *schweschders*?"

Sarah shook her head. "*Nee*, I don't have any. *Mamm* had trouble having me. I was the only *boppli*."

Martha was full of concern. "Where are you staying now?"

Sarah held a tissue to her eyes, and Martha was afraid that her question might have promoted a fresh flood of tears. "I have nowhere to stay! *Gott* has abandoned me."

"*Nee, nee*," Martha hurried to say. "*Gott* hasn't abandoned you. You can stay with my *familye* until you figure things out." Martha thought of her own *mudder's* possible reaction to Sarah, and so added, "Or perhaps another *familye* in my community. But you do have somewhere to stay now. *Gott* has brought me to you."

Sarah's face brightened. "*Jah*, I suppose He has."

"When I leave here, I'll leave my *familye's* name with the police officers for you. And just in case they don't give it to you, you'll remember the name *Miller*, won't you?"

"*Jah*." Sarah had stopped crying and had some color back in her cheeks. "*Denki*, Martha, *denki* so much. I feel so much better now."

Martha looked around the room. She realized that she was sitting in a holding cell at a police station, all bars and concrete, cold and frightening, and she was under arrest. Yet her spirits lifted, as she was sure that *Gott* had led her there to help Sarah.

The rest of the afternoon seemed to pass in a flash, and Martha felt detached from the whole proceedings. It was as if she were having a dream from which she was unable to awake.

At her request, the officers allowed Martha to make a phone call. Martha sat under the harsh light of low-hanging fluorescent lights in a cold, gray office chair beside a stark, metal desk in the middle of a room filled with police officers at similar metal desks, while the officer called the Hostetler barn. Martha looked around the room. The plaster was peeling off the walls, which were painted in two shades of a most unpleasant green. The floor was tiled in two more horrible shades of green. The smell of coffee filled the air, but it was not a welcoming scent. Rather, it was intimidating. Everything about the room was intimidating.

The officer handed the phone to Martha, but there was no answer. "Could you please try one more time?" she asked the officer.

"Once more," he said. He tried again, but there was still no answer.

Martha was then taken to another man who spoke for some time, but by then, she was in a daze.

Finally, one of the officers shoved something in front of her to sign. She read it—it said she agreed to be present for hearings. After she signed it, the officer said, "You can go now."

"But what about bail?" Martha knew nothing of arrest procedures, except for the fact that people usually had to pay bail.

"You're out on ROR."

When Martha looked up at him, puzzled, he explained. "You are released on your own recognizance. You've agreed in writing to appear at all proceedings. ROR means you don't have to post any money and you're not required to check in." He handed Martha a paper bag with her belongings. "The stolen purse in your possession has been kept as evidence." As Martha stood looking at him, he added, "Do you have enough money for a taxi home?"

Martha nodded, and the policeman walked off, saying, "Make sure you get a lawyer," over his shoulder before he left.

Martha had no idea how she got home to her apartment. Once she was inside, she locked the door behind her and made a cup of hot meadow tea. She sat and sipped it, shivering despite the fact that the afternoon was warm. Sheryl was supposed to be back by now, but there was no sign of her. Martha had no idea if Sheryl was still being detained at the police station. She had asked the police officers about Sheryl, but they had refused to tell her anything.

After the meadow tea, Martha's head cleared somewhat. She did not want her *familye* to know that she had been arrested for stealing. Despite the fact that she was innocent, she felt ashamed. She had so wanted to make her way in the *Englisch* world, and her *mudder*, if she heard what happened, would insist that she return home at once.

There was only one thing for it: she would have to call Moses.

Martha took her phone out of the paper bag and called the Hostetler barn. *Please pick up, please pick up*, she repeated over and over again. It rang out twice. "Please *Gott*, please *Gott*, let someone answer," she said aloud. Finally, on the third try, she heard Moses's voice.

"Moses!" Martha all but yelled down the phone.

"What's happened? Is something wrong?"

"Yes." Martha only managed to get the one word out before collapsing into a flood of tears. Try as she might, she was unable to stop crying, but sobbed and sobbed, only pausing to blow her nose loudly, and all the while, Moses was still on the phone.

"I'll be right there." At least that's what she thought Moses said, and the line went dead. Martha wondered what to do, and after a while called back, but there was no answer, so she assumed he was on the way.

Martha paced up and down the apartment until Moses arrived, and it was all she could do not to fling herself at him and sob on his shoulder.

Moses's face was white and drawn. "What's happened?"

"I was arrested," Martha blurted.

Moses jaw dropped open. "Now come and sit down. I'll make you some hot tea and you can tell me all about it. I know you don't like sugar in your tea, but it will help with the shock."

Martha allowed herself to be led to the sofa, and as Moses headed for the kitchen, she called out, "The sugar's in the salt container."

Moses returned with the tea and wouldn't let Martha speak until she'd sipped some. "Now, tell me all about it."

Martha told Moses how she had been arrested for stealing, how the police had searched the place, and that they had accused her of being in a retail theft organization with Sheryl.

Moses looked thoughtful. "And who is in this supposed retail theft organization?"

Martha shrugged. "Just me, I think, oh, and Sheryl obviously. The police officers said they found thousands of dollars' worth of stolen designer clothes and purses, and expensive jewelry too, right here in this apartment."

"You told them you had nothing to do with it, obviously."

"Yes." Martha nodded vehemently, but that made her head hurt. "They didn't believe me. I told them I'd only borrowed clothes from Sheryl. Anyway, they said if I told them all I knew, I'd get a lesser sentence, but I'd already told them everything I knew, and they didn't believe me." Martha felt she would cry again, but there were no more tears left. Instead, her head throbbed horribly.

"You need a lawyer."

Martha nodded. "Ouch, Moses, I've suddenly got a crashing headache. Could you please get me some Advil? There's some in the bathroom."

Moses hurried off to find the Advil, while Martha was left to sit there and consider how blessed she was to have such a friend as Moses. She felt safe and protected when Moses was around. Even the arrest didn't seem so frightening now that Moses was going to help.

Moses returned with Advil and a glass of water. "Don't worry, Martha. I'll take care of everything. I'll find you a *gut* lawyer. I assume you don't want your *familye* to know?"

Martha winced. "It's just *Mamm*. She'd make me come home at once, and I'd lose my new chocolate contract. I'd like to tell my *schweschders* and my *daed*, but they wouldn't be able to keep it from *Mamm*. Can it just be our secret for the moment?"

"Of course." Moses smiled at her tenderly, and took her hand in his, patting it gently.

Martha looked up into his thoughtful, blue eyes and felt that all was well with the world, with Moses there to care for her.

Chapter Eighteen

Sheryl had not returned, and Martha had no idea where she was. She had called her cell repeatedly, but it appeared to be turned off. Martha had no idea if Sheryl was paying the rent, or what was going on. She would need to speak to her soon.

All Martha could do was continue her work as a short order cook, and try to raise funds to pay for the lawyer by selling chocolates at the upcoming farmers' market. The market was open every Saturday, but she hadn't been able to get there for some time. Now she needed every cent. She had no idea how much lawyers cost, apart from the fact that they were sure to be horribly expensive.

Martha was melting chocolate over a water bath when there was a knock at the door. She hurried to the door, hoping it was Sheryl, although Sheryl did, of course, have her own key. "Sheryl," she said hopefully, opening the door.

"Not last time I looked. Hey, you don't look

happy to see me." Gary was standing in the doorway, dressed in better clothes than the usual casual clothes he wore around the apartment.

"Oh, Gary, come in. Come to the kitchen and talk. I'm tempering chocolate."

"You're what?"

Martha beckoned to Gary, and hurried back into the kitchen.

"I've been away at a conference, just in case you were wondering where I was. Did you miss me?"

Martha looked over her shoulder. "Oh, you were away?"

Gary looked crestfallen. "Well, that answers my question. Where's Sheryl?" He reached over to a small bowl and picked up some chocolate, which he shoved into his mouth.

"No, Gary!" Martha said sharply. "That's the seed. You can't eat it."

"It tastes like chocolate to me, not seeds," Gary said in a confused voice through a mouthful of chocolate.

Martha shook her head. "No, I mean yes, it's called the *seed* but it's about a quarter of the chocolate. I have to add it in later. Don't touch any more."

Gary shrugged. "Fine, if that's how you feel. So anyway, where's Sheryl?"

"I haven't seen her since I was arrested," Martha said without thinking.

"What?" Gary's voice rose to a shriek. "Did you say *arrested*?"

"Yes, so I'm making chocolates to pay for my lawyer. I'd make you some coffee and sit down and talk, but I've started tempering the chocolate for the cherries and I can't stop now or I'll have to do the whole thing all over again." Martha was flustered; having interruptions while tempering chocolate was bad at the best of times, but now she'd have to explain the whole situation to Gary. "I really have to concentrate, 'cause even a small amount of water can make the chocolate seize. I'll tell you everything, but I'll have to do this while I talk, if that's okay."

"Sure." Gary walked over to her. "Does it bother you if I watch?"

"No, that's fine." Martha took a deep breath. "The police said that Sheryl's been stealing thousands of dollars' worth of designer dresses and purses, and they think she must be running an organization and that I'm part of it, 'cause when they came with the search warrant, I was wearing stolen clothes."

"Hey man, that's heavy."

Martha looked up at him, and then stirred the chocolate. "I didn't know they were stolen, obviously. I had no idea Sheryl was stealing things. The police don't believe me, of course."

"Did you tell them you were a simple Amish girl unfamiliar with the ways of the world and straight off the farm?"

Martha looked up from the digital probe thermometer and shot Gary a sharp look, but he didn't appear to be joking. In fact, he looked quite serious.

"I told them I was on *rumspringa* and that I'm Amish, but they didn't seem to think that made any difference. So I was arrested and I haven't seen Sheryl since."

Gary let out a long whistle. "Serious. You do have a lawyer, don't you?"

Martha put the thermometer down and shook her head. "Not yet, Moses is getting a lawyer for me."

Gary grunted. "Moses, your Amish boyfriend." It was a statement rather than a question.

Martha shook her head. "*Nee*, he's not my boyfriend." As soon as the words were out, she wished she had avoided the subject. She did not want to encourage Gary. She had given up any idea of having him as an *Englisch* boyfriend. Now he might see her saying she wasn't dating Moses as an open invitation to pursue matters further.

"Anyway," she continued, "that's why I'm making these chocolates, to pay for the lawyer. I can't imagine a lawyer would be cheap."

"That's for sure. So who are you selling these chocolates to?"

"Oh, didn't I tell you? The farmers' markets. I used to go there quite often. That's how I saved up enough money for the rent here."

"Wouldn't your family pay for the lawyer?"

"*Nee, nee,*" Martha said, and then amended it. "No, no, I don't want my *familye* to know. My *mudder*, err, mother, would be most upset and she'd force me to go home immediately. I don't want to go home until I've finished my *rumspringa,* especially now that I have that chocolate contract in place."

Martha turned her attention to adding the seed to the mixture and stirring it with a spatula.

"So you *are* going home then?" Gary said, after a few moments.

Martha looked at Gary. "What do you mean?"

"I thought you had no intention of returning to the Amish at all, and now you're saying you'll go home after you finish your *rumspringa*."

Martha stopped dipping a small strip of parchment paper into the chocolate, and stared at Gary. "I said that?" She thought over her words. Did she really intend to return home? Or did she wish to remain an *Englischer*? *My subconscious mind clearly thought I was intending to return home*, she thought. Martha was confused, so confused in fact, that she stared at Gary so long trying to make sense of her thoughts that the chocolate cooled too much and went hard, and she had to start the tempering process all over again.

Chapter Nineteen

Martha and Gary arrived in Gary's car early in the morning at the farmers' market. Martha had accepted Gary's offer to help at the markets as she was so overwrought with everything that had been happening. There had still been no word from Sheryl, but Martha had visited the leasing agent, who had informed her that Sheryl's rent was up to date and in advance by one month. Martha figured that gave her a little breathing space.

Martha usually enjoyed her day at the markets, with its family friendly and energetic atmosphere, but she was feeling quite down about the whole situation of her arrest. She was also frustrated by the injustice of it all. There was a good chance she could go to jail, but she couldn't let herself think about that for now. *Gott* knew she was innocent, and *Gott* was the supreme judge.

The open air market was held every Saturday and attracted vendors of all descriptions selling their products: food, crafts, quilts, art, and candles to name but a few. Vendors set up either side of the pathway, and Martha was glad that Gary was there to help her put up the gazebo folding tent.

Soon there were bright blue tents lining both sides of the pathway, and Martha was pleased to see she was again between a bakery and an organic vegetable grower. That would mean people were thinking about food when they reached her stall. She herself was thinking about food. The aroma of freshly baked bread was tantalizing, and reminded her of home, and of the fact that she hadn't had breakfast.

Gary did prove to be of help, although he was quite absent-minded at times. He took out the cartons of chocolates as Martha had instructed and helped her set them up. The official time for the market to start was still half an hour away, but people were already drifting through. Although Martha had allowed herself plenty of time, she felt she was rushing to set up in time. She was grateful for Gary's help, but sometimes doing things oneself was the fastest way to get things done; instructing took time.

"Rebecca!" Martha saw Rebecca, the youngest of the four Miller sisters, approach. The two of them had always been close, just as Hannah and Esther had always been close. Martha hugged Rebecca and Rebecca returned her hug, but then when they pulled away, Rebecca's eyebrows were raised. It was not usual in Amish communities to show affection, at least not in public.

"You're so *Englisch* now," Rebecca said, looking

Martha up and down. Before Martha could reply, she added, "And I really miss you. *Mamm's* got a steady stream of *menner* coming to the *haus*. She wants to get me married off as soon as possible."

Martha laughed. "*Jah*, she's always been like that."

"*Jah*, but I'm the only *maidel* left at home, so she's turned all her attention to me."

Rebecca looked so downcast that Martha tried to cheer her up. "Come on, then, have a chocolate. *Denki* for helping me too."

"I always help you at the markets, Martha." Rebecca's mouth was still turned down at the sides.

Martha had forgotten about Gary, who was standing behind the stall. "Oh, Rebecca, this is Gary. He lives in the apartment above me."

The two exchanged greetings, and then Rebecca leaned in close to Martha and whispered, "Is he *de bo*?"

"*Nee, nee*, he's not my boyfriend," Martha whispered hurriedly, glancing at Gary, who was clearly pretending he wasn't listening, but clearly was.

"What's happening with Moses then?" Rebecca whispered, while Gary took a step closer, while looking off into the distance.

"Nothing, nothing at all." Martha gave her *schweschder* a stern look.

"This is *me* you're talking to," Rebecca whispered, but more loudly this time. "Don't try to fool me. I'm not *ferhoodled*! I know you too well."

Martha held up her hands in exasperation, but then her first customer for the day arrived, which saved her from Rebecca's questions. Martha tried to concentrate on the customer's questions, but she kept one ear on Rebecca, who was now questioning Gary.

When the customer left, Martha turned to Gary. "Thank you so much for bringing me here and helping me set up. Now that Rebecca's here, I'll be right for some time, if you want to go off and explore the markets."

Gary scratched his head, while he apparently thought over her suggestion. "Okay, sure. I'll come back from time to time to see if you need help."

Martha made to thank him but Rebecca spoke first. "See that cream colored tent over there?" She pointed, and Gary nodded. "They have the best apple butter, and apple snitz, and apple cider too."

Gary's face lighted up and he hurried away. "So, tell me what's going on with Moses now," Rebecca demanded, her hands on her hips.

"Nothing's going on with Moses, truly."

"But you like him, don't you?"

"*Jah*." Martha nodded furiously. "But he'll never leave the Amish."

Rebecca shrugged. "So? Surely that's a *gut* thing."

Martha was exasperated. "I don't know why no one takes me seriously, not even my own *familye*. I've said for ages that I was going to be *Englisch*, and not come back to the Amish, but have a chocolate business."

Martha expected Rebecca to be annoyed, but she simply said, "You can have a chocolate business *and* be Amish."

"Yes, but…" Martha's voice trailed away.

"So, what's it like being *Englisch*?"

Martha thought for a moment. "Well, if something goes wrong, there's really no one to call on for help. I mean, you could ask a neighbor or a friend, and they might give some sympathy or help a little, but there's no certainty of complete help like you get from the community. You have to go out to a store to buy milk and eggs, plus it's very lonely too. I wasn't expecting that. There's a feeling of isolation. There's an emphasis on how you look and even I've caught myself looking in shop windows at my reflection lately, even though the *Englisch* have mirrors everywhere. There's a big emphasis on personal appearance."

Martha would have gone on, but Rebecca stopped her. "Is there anything *gut* about being *Englisch*?"

Martha rubbed her chin. "Well, there's the freedom, and cars are much faster than buggies."

"Do you have a license to drive a car?" Rebecca popped a chocolate-coated cherry into her mouth.

"Well, no."

"So you have to be driven anyway, and that's the same as being Amish, isn't it?"

Martha had to admit that Rebecca was right. Still, there must be good things about being *Englisch*, and, as Martha served the next few customers, she tried to think what they were.

"I wonder why that is," Rebecca said to herself, after a large group of customers had left.

"What's that?"

"The customers never come one at a time. There

are no customers for a while, then they all come at once."

Martha laughed. "That's true, but at least it gives us a bit of a break. Anyway, how are Hannah's twins?"

"Oh they're so cute," Rebecca gushed. "Hannah wants you to come and see them again soon. You will, won't you?"

"Of course." Martha was hit with pangs of guilt, as her visits to Hannah and her *bopplin* had been infrequent. Had she still been living at home, she would have visited Hannah and the *bopplin* every day.

Martha had just finished wrapping chocolates for another customer, when Rebecca tugged on her arm and nodded to her left. Martha followed the direction of her gaze and saw Moses approaching.

Martha was hit with a sudden coldness followed by dizziness, and an unpleasant churning in her stomach. Laura, the waitress from work, was walking with Moses. Laura had not mentioned Moses to her lately, so Martha had thought she had lost interest in him.

The two walked over to Martha's stall, smiling. Martha introduced Rebecca to Laura. "I found Laura at the markets," Moses said pointedly.

Martha wondered if he'd said that to reassure her that the two of them had not come to the markets together. *Still, I'm not dating Moses*, she thought, *so why would he feel it necessary to say that? Or perhaps he is interested in her and doesn't want anyone to suspect.* Martha found it hard to think clearly with Moses and Laura standing opposite her, looking for all the world like a happy couple.

While Martha was trying to clear her head, Gary appeared. He was clutching a large jar and looking awfully pleased with himself. "Look, I bought some Sweet Pumpkin Hummus," he announced. "Who'd have thought that there was such a thing? Oh hi, guys." He nodded to Moses and Laura. "Did you come here together? Are you an item?"

Moses and Laura both looked shocked. "No, no," they said in unison. "I just happened to see Laura when I arrived," Moses added, "so we came looking for Martha."

Martha was surprised at Gary's lack of tact, but grateful that his questions had brought out the answer that Moses and Laura were not dating. She breathed a sigh of relief.

Moses turned to Martha and smiled. She melted under his smile, and suddenly, all felt right with her world again. "Can I have a word with you?" he asked. "Perhaps Rebecca can mind the stall for a moment."

Martha nodded. "And Gary, can you please help Rebecca?"

Moses raised an eyebrow. "Gary's here helping me today," Martha explained, but then saw a cloud pass over Moses's face. *Oh no, he's jealous*, she thought. *He must think that Gary and I are more than just friends*.

"I'll help too," Laura said, casting a sidelong glance at Gary, a glance that didn't escape Martha's notice. Martha smiled to herself and thanked Laura.

"Come, let's get *kaffi*," Moses said, leading Martha away. They walked in companionable silence under a pleasant canopy of trees, which provided welcome relief from the sun. Moses kept walking, away from the markets.

"Where are we going?"

"Just a little grocery store that's also a café," Moses said, "It's close to the markets and has better *kaffi*. I thought we could have lunch."

"That's a *gut* idea, and we can avoid any Amish people," Martha said.

Moses looked at her and raised his eyebrows.

"Well, I feel a little strange wearing *Englisch* clothes," Martha said. "I don't want to answer questions about *rumspringa*."

Moses nodded, but didn't answer, as they had arrived at the café. He opened the door for Martha to enter, and she was immediately struck by the cheerful atmosphere of the little café. The walls were painted mint green, and some of the tables were glass-topped wood, while others were covered with pink tablecloths. There were pretty flowers on every table. Pine shelves lined the walls, and they were filled with all manner of produce, in bottles with brightly colored lids. Other walls had brightly colored abstract paintings. Martha's spirits were lifted just by being in the place.

As soon as she took her seat, Moses asked, "Has there been any word from Sheryl?"

Martha shook her head. "*Nee*, and I'm quite worried. The police wouldn't keep her locked up all this time, would they?"

It was Moses's turn to shake his head. "They

wouldn't, but it's strange that she hasn't contacted you."

"Perhaps she's embarrassed," Martha said, enjoying Moses's proximity, and the fact that she had him all to herself, at least for lunch. "So you didn't come to the markets with Laura?" Martha was at once dismayed by her words, as she had not wished to voice her concerns aloud.

Moses merely smiled. "Are you jealous?"

"Of course not." Martha tried to fix him with a stern and convincing look.

"And Gary's helping you today?" he asked.

"Yes." Martha smiled. "Are *you* jealous?"

"*Jah*, as a matter of fact, I am."

Martha's mouth fell open. She had no idea that Moses was jealous, and had even less idea that he would actually admit to it. She did not know how to respond, so stared at the menu. When Moses did not speak, Martha considered how she had felt when she was jealous over Laura, so thought that the right thing to do would be to set Moses straight. "He's just a friend, and that's all." She avoided Gary's eyes when she spoke. "I am hoping he and Laura will start dating."

She risked a glance at Moses, and he was smiling. "Let's order lunch."

Martha's stomach growled as if on cue. "I've haven't had breakfast."

Moses frowned. "That's not *gut*, Martha. You mustn't skip meals, especially with a hard day's work ahead of you."

Martha smiled. It was nice that Moses cared for her wellbeing. Her feelings for him were strong, but could she go back to the Amish and stay there forever? The growling of her stomach turned her thoughts, for now, to food. Martha ordered a black-bean-and-cheese quesadilla with homemade guacamole, and Moses, fishermen's stew. They both ordered lemonade to go with their meal, and *kaffi* to come with the raspberry lavender pies afterward.

As soon as the waiter left, Moses said, "I have a lawyer for you."

"You do? How much will he cost? I still have some money I've saved, and I'm hoping to do well today, too."

Moses shook his head. "*Nee*, Martha." He laid his big hand over hers. Vibrations ran all through Martha and a warm, tingly feeling settled over her like a spring cloud. "I'll be paying for your lawyer," he added, patting her hand gently.

"But you can't! We're not married," Martha blurted, much to her own embarrassment. *Why can't I think before I speak?* she silently berated herself, feeling her face grow hot, and the tips of her ears burn. She wished she could sink right through the floor.

"Well, unless you're planning to marry anyone else soon, I hope you'll allow me to pay for your lawyer." When Martha didn't reply, he added, "You're my closest friend, and I want you to allow me to do this for you."

Martha thought for a bit. "Thank you, Moses. That's very *gut* of you, and I appreciate it. I really should ask my *daed* to pay for it, though, as it sounds like it's going to be expensive." The waiter returned and deposited a glass of lemonade in front of each of them. When he had left, Moses said, "*Nee*, Martha, you can't tell your *familye*, or your *mudder* will force you to move back home."

Martha was shocked. "But isn't that what you want, Moses?"

Moses smiled, and his eyes were full of warmth, and something else, but Martha did not know what. "Of course I want you home. But *rumspringa* is all about deciding for yourself. I wouldn't want you just because you felt obligated. I'd want you to come home to stay forever only if that's what you wanted with your whole heart."

Martha met Moses's eyes and something passed between them. She held his gaze and felt unable to look away. Martha knew there was more to his words than on the surface, that Moses meant more than her returning to the Miller *haus*.

Chapter Twenty

Martha and Moses arrived at the lawyer's offices. Moses had assured her that the lawyer was a good one, and Martha knew that Moses would have been careful in that regard. However, she had expected to find the lawyer in a tall building, all steel and glass, so was surprised when the taxi pulled up outside a red brick and stone, Georgian-style building. The fact that the lawn needed mowing gave Martha pause. There was a statue of Justice outside the porch, and that would have been fine, had not the statue been leaning to one side. That statue and the sign saying "William Griffits, Attorney at Law" were the only clues that this was, in fact, the office of a lawyer.

Martha looked down the street. It was well kept, with nicely manicured lawns, unlike the lawyer's, and had a variety of Georgian homes. The building next to the lawyer's building was white with pretty, green shutters on the windows.

As she approached the front steps, Martha felt a

rush of anxiety. Moses held the door for her and she walked in. There was no one else in the waiting room, but Moses had told her that he had chosen the appointment time of 9 a.m. so that they would not be kept waiting. The elderly and efficient-looking receptionist looked up at them from behind her massive, timber desk.

"Martha Miller to see Mr. Griffits," Moses announced. Martha was glad that Moses had spoken. In fact, she was glad that Moses had arranged absolutely everything pertaining to the lawyer for her. She was so nervous and upset that she was sure that she wouldn't have been able to speak at all. She looked to Moses for reassurance and he smiled at her.

"Mr. Griffits will be with you in a minute," the receptionist said automatically, as if she were reciting a dull poem. "Please take a seat."

Martha sat down and looked around her. The carpet was floral, and looked very old indeed. It was slightly worn around the edges. The waiting room was drab and had little, if any, natural light. The fluorescent light overhead flickered and Martha was sure it would give her a headache. Her temples were already beginning to pound.

Soon there was the distant sound of a door opening, and an elderly man came down the hallway toward them. He was bent over, and appeared to have difficulty walking even with his walking stick, which Martha noticed was very fancy with a shining silver-and-white handle. His white, bushy eyebrows swooped upward to meet high in the middle of his forehead, giving him an expression of constant surprise. When he reached the pair, he bent over Martha and said, "Miss Miller, please come in." His voice was booming, and seemed out of place, given his fragile appearance.

Martha and Moses stood up to follow him, and follow him they did, all the way down the long corridor, and at a very slow pace. Mr. Griffits opened the door to his office and nodded to them to enter.

Martha at once saw that the room was oversized, and she hurried to sit in one of the equally oversized, brown, leather chairs, which creaked and crackled as she lowered herself into it. The walls were yellowing beige, and Martha wondered for a moment if they were moldy, as the smell of damp hung in the air.

Moses took the other chair, and Mr. Griffits finally made his way to his large wooden chair and sat down on it with obvious relief. He then drank some water from a nearby glass, and then sneezed violently.

"As you would be aware," he began, "I am Mr. Griffits."

"Oh yes, Mr. Griffiths," Martha said.

Mr. Griffits fixed his gleaming eyes on her. "I am not Mr. Griffiths, but rather, Mr. Griffits," he said sternly.

"Oh yes, I knew that, Mr. Griffiths, *err* Griffits, Griffits," Martha stammered, fighting back the urge to laugh nervously. "I'm just very anxious."

Mr. Griffits smiled thinly. "There is no need to be anxious. I have practiced law for over forty years. I provide an aggressive defense for all matters including theft."

"But I didn't do it," Martha said.

"There is one thing I tell my clients," Mr. Griffits said in his booming voice, "and you would do well to heed it. The law has nothing to do with justice. Do you understand?"

Martha nodded, although she didn't quite understand, truth be told.

"Mr. Hostetler has given me an overview of the situation. Now be so kind as to give me your version of events."

Martha told him the whole story. She was nervous at first, but Mr. Griffits looked up from his notes from time to time and nodded encouragingly, so she began to relax somewhat.

"When do you intend to return home from *rumspringa* to your community?" was his first question, after she had finished speaking.

Of all questions, that was the one that Martha could not answer, especially not in front of Moses.

"Um, I'm not sure," Martha said, looking away from him at the thick and aged volumes of leather-bound legal books on the overburdened bookshelves.

"You must return home soon," the lawyer advised.

"But I haven't finished *rumspringa*," Martha said, worried where this was heading.

"No matter." Mr. Griffits waved a hand at her dismissively. "You will return home soon, and, more importantly, wear Amish clothes to all and any court hearings." Martha made to speak, but Mr. Griffits waved his hand at her again. "It should not be so, but appearances *do* matter in a court of law. Oh, if only that were not the case. But it is," he boomed, "and so you will appear dressed in your Amish clothes in court. Is that understood?"

Martha nodded meekly.

"Further," he continued, "you are to have nothing to do with Sheryl Garner. If she calls, you do not accept her call. If you see her on the street, you cross it to avoid her. You do not speak to her under any circumstances. You are to move out of her apartment as soon as possible."

"I will," Martha said in a small voice. "What do you think my chances are? My chances of being found not guilty, I mean."

Mr. Griffits raised his eyebrows even higher than appeared possible. "Sheryl Garner has a lengthy criminal record."

Martha and Moses both gasped at the disclosure.

"You answered her newspaper advertisement to rent a room in her apartment, having not known her prior to that date. You, an innocent young Amish woman, naive to the ways of the world, and having no non-Amish clothes, simply borrowed clothing from Sheryl at her insistence during your first foray out of your sheltered community." Mr. Griffits clasped his hands together with excitement. "The police have no evidence that will stand up to examination. I cannot make any promises, Miss Miller, for the law is a fickle beast, but I would not lose any sleep over this matter if I were you. I have won serious cases, and this case, although it has caused you great concern, is quite straightforward. Do not worry."

Mr. Griffits stood up, which Martha took as their cue to leave. He opened the door for them, and they walked through. The receptionist was on the phone, and there were two people in the waiting room.

Moses turned to Martha as soon as they were outside, on the porch. "Feel better now?"

"Oh yes." Martha breathed a long sigh of relief. "He doesn't seem worried at all."

"Yes, he'll win the case for you. There's no need to worry, Martha, truly, but you must do as he says."

As Martha lay in her bed that night, she felt relieved that her lawyer appeared confident that she would win her case, but she did not want to return home, not yet. If she went home now, she would never be sure that she did so entirely willingly. She needed to decide once and for all whether she wanted to be Amish or *Englisch*, as she would have to live with that decision for the rest of her life. Also, if she returned home now, her *mudder* would find out that she was charged with theft, and would never let her continue her *rumspringa* at a later date. There seemed to be no solution in sight. Martha tossed and turned, and had not a wink of sleep until she turned the whole matter over to *Gott*, at least for the night.

Chapter Twenty-One

Martha had been terribly stressed the past few weeks. To prevent the criminal charges occupying Martha's mind at all hours of the day, Moses had suggested they get a bus out to the lake and take a scenic boat tour. When they arrived, the tour guide, a round man with a bright tan, and wearing a mint, cable-knit sweater, suggested the pair of them pop down to the store and grab ice creams, to pass the time until the boat's departure.

Now she stood by the lake, jotting down the sun reflecting off the water in her mind, so she might never forget the beautiful sight, as Moses returned with their ice creams. He had ordered the flavors of chocolate chip and strawberry. Martha picked the strawberry, and now she and Moses were on the boat, pulling away from the shore, with the sun on their backs.

"*Denki* so much for doing this," she said to Moses, "I've just been so stressed with everything that's been going on. I can't believe how silly I've been, how I failed even to consider where Sheryl was finding all the clothes and jewelry that she gave me to wear. In hindsight, it's so obvious now."

"Don't be so hard on yourself," Moses replied, wiping the crumbs from the ice cream cone off his hands, pants, and the collar of his shirt. "You trust people easily, Martha. It's not a bad thing. In fact, it's a very good thing. I'm sure the charges will be dropped in time, and so the worst thing to come out of this is just a tough lesson for you to take on board and consider."

"I suppose you're right."

Martha shivered as the cool lake breeze pressed into her bare arms. She missed the heavy cloak that all Amish girls wore in the autumn and winter seasons, and missed the feel of sturdy wool to protect her against the elements. Moses must have noticed her trembling, for he wrapped his arm around her shoulder and pulled her tight. His body felt so strong. Martha supposed all the farm work he did could not be for nothing, and she could not help but let a blush spread over her cheeks.

"How is, err, what is his name again?" said Moses.

"Gary?" replied Martha, as a stern expression crept over Moses's face. She wondered why her reply would annoy him, when he had asked the question in the first place. *Although*, she thought, *I did say Gary's name very quickly. Perhaps Moses was expecting me to take more time.* "Gary is really the only *mann*

I know who you don't know too well," she added, awkwardly.

Before Moses could reply, the scenic tour guide in the cable-knit sweater appeared, to ask if everything was okay. "And you are sure there is nothing I can get for the beautiful young couple?" he finished.

"Oh," replied Martha, feeling the blush on her cheeks deepen, "We're not a couple." That only made Moses frown more, and she felt like nothing was going right for her of late. "But thank you for asking."

"You never answered my question," said Moses, removing his hand from Martha's shoulder and fiddling with the cuffs on his plain white shirt.

"He's fine, I believe. Although I think he was very shocked to hear about Sheryl. He said if he'd known what she was doing, he would have stepped in and told her to not involve me."

"How kind of him."

"Is anything the matter?"

"No, no." Moses smiled now. "I'm sorry, Martha. I brought you out here to distract you from Sheryl and the charges, not to bring them up again and again."

"I don't mind all that much. It does help to talk about it, and I wouldn't want to involve anybody else in my mess."

"Just involve me?"

"I'm sorry," said Martha, wishing even more for her heavy woolen cloak now. She felt so warm and safe in that coat, but here, with Moses and the lake stretching before her, she felt terribly exposed.

"*Nee*! I'm glad you involved me, Martha. You

know I'm always here for you, no matter what. I feel like I'm making a complete mess of this."

"That's exactly how I feel," Martha said, and the pair of them laughed. "What a sorry sight we make today, Moses. At least we had ice cream. A day is never truly bad if you get to eat ice cream."

"Ah, wise words from Martha Miller. Do you have any more wisdom to impart to me? I had best learn all I can before you…"

"Before I?"

"Marry, I suppose." Now it was Moses's turn to blush. "I don't know. Despite what you said the other day, I just thought you might be thinking of Gary as a… Here I go, messing it all up again. Have you heard from Hannah or Esther or Rebecca? I bet you miss your *schweschders* a lot."

Martha did not reply for a minute or so. She looked searchingly across the lake, to the vegetation growing on the damp shore. The bushes rustled in the lake breeze, while the sunlight filtered through the trees, dancing across the rippling water. She felt so bad for poor Moses, as her head felt all over the place today, and now she missed her *schweschders* terribly. She wondered where they were at this exact moment, and if they felt as well and happy as she currently felt scared and confused. Her two older *schweschders*, Hannah and Esther, were always the most sensible of the four, so she supposed they were fine. Her little *schweschder*, Rebecca, was still at home, and would no doubt be helping their mother with the chores, and not accepting stolen goods from a thieving roommate. She sighed.

"It is a little strange, isn't it? You grow up with someone, spend all your time with them, laughing and working and all the rest, and suddenly they're gone and you can't even feel sorry about it, because both Hannah and Esther are blissfully married. To your *bruders*, no less! I wonder if our parents ever saw that coming."

"Parents usually do."

"That's true. Although, I think my *mudder* wanted both Hannah and Esther to marry other *menner*. Not that she was upset about them marrying your *bruders*, of course," Martha hastened to add.

Martha looked over to Moses now. He was very handsome, even more so in the golden sunlight, with the lake twinkling in the background. She knew her *schweschders* married his *bruders* for their kindness and their warmth, and not for their looks, but their bronzed skin and crooked smiles no doubt sweetened the deal. Martha smiled guiltily at the very thought. She felt very wicked for thinking such things.

"So your *mudder* now approves of my *familye*?" inquired Moses, his face beaming at the thought. "I suppose our *familye*s must now like each other a great deal, if two of my *bruders* have married two of your *schweschders*. I wonder what they'd all say if they could see us today, out here on this beautiful lake, in this beautiful boat, with the sun rising above us."

Martha laughed. "They'd probably say, 'Here we go again! Another Miller *schweschder* is going to marry another Hostetler *bruder*.' That's quite the thought, isn't it?"

"That is," replied Moses, a large grin spreading over his handsome face.

Chapter Twenty-Two

"Did you say Mr. Griffiths?" Gary had just dropped by with six brownie batter donuts, which he proceeded to stuff in his mouth rather quickly after Martha refused one.

"His name is Mr. Griffits, actually. Have you heard of him?"

"Oh, I thought his name was Griffiths, but yes, I've heard of him, if he's elderly and kind of stooped over, and has a very loud voice and huge, bushy eyebrows?" Gary attempted to mime bushy eyebrows.

Martha smiled. "That's him."

"He's famous!" Gary exclaimed. "He gets those really bad criminals off their charges. How on earth can you afford him?"

Marta's smile at once turned into a frown. "He's expensive?"

Gary nodded, and pointed to his mouth to indicate that he couldn't speak as it was full of donuts. He finally spoke when his mouth was half empty.

"Well, he's pretty famous. He's on TV all the time," he managed to say.

Martha's stomach clenched. How much was Moses paying this man? She felt horribly guilty for placing such a burden on Moses.

"So that's why you're moving out then, is it?" Gary asked.

Martha moved across to the sofas and sat down on one. Gary followed and sat opposite her. "Yes, Mr. Griffits advised me to avoid Sheryl, not that I think she'll ever come back, and he said I should move back home soon."

"Hey, if you have to avoid Sheryl, you can rent my spare room."

Martha gasped. "Oh thank you for the kind thought, Gary, but that wouldn't be right."

Gary looked offended. "It would all be above board and all that, no funny business." His offended expression changed to one of hurt. "We *Englischers,* or whatever you call us, do that all the time, boys and girls renting together. They don't even have to be friends."

Martha forced a smile. "You're a good friend, Gary, but I couldn't."

Gary pouted. "You're not Amish anymore."

"But I *am* Amish. I've just been on *rumspringa.*" Martha inhaled sharply. The fact she had said that surprised her.

Gary pulled a long face. "But we'll still be friends, won't we? You'll come back and see me—and Laura too?"

"Of course I will. Actually, I gave notice at work this morning, but Laura wasn't there. I'll have to tell her what's happening too."

"I'll tell her if you like," Gary said. "We're having dinner tonight." As soon as his words were out, his face went beet red, and he stood up and shuffled over to the window.

Martha followed him. "Gary, are you and Laura dating?"

Gary nodded, and smiled shyly.

"Gary, that's *wunderbar*, err, wonderful! I'm so pleased for both of you." Martha felt a little guilty that part of her pleasure was for the fact that Laura had clearly given up her previous little crush on Moses.

Gary was still blushing furiously, so Martha figured he must really like Laura. After his disclosure, Gary for once seemed at a loss for words, so hurried to the door after putting the last brownie batter donut in his mouth.

After she had shown him out, Martha made her way to the kitchen, but was only half way there when there was a knock at the door. Figuring Gary had forgotten to tell her something, Martha hurried back to the door and opened it.

To her dismay, a man and a woman were standing outside the door, looking quite serious. Martha's stomach twisted. Were these plain-clothes police officers coming to take her in for more questioning?

"Martha Miller?" the man said.

"Yes," Martha said in small, frightened voice, trying not to burst into tears.

"We're Sheryl Graber's parents," the man said. "May we come in and talk to you please?"

Martha hesitated a moment, being somewhat in shock. Her sense of relief that they were not police officers was fleeting, for Mr. Griffits had said she must have no contact with Sheryl—but surely that would not extend to Sheryl's parents?

"Is Sheryl with you?" she asked, standing in the doorway.

"No, she isn't," the woman said.

Martha stood aside. "Please come in." She showed them to the sofa. "Please sit down. Would you like a cup of coffee, or hot tea?"

Mrs. Garner, who was wringing her hands nervously, spoke up. "I'd like hot tea please, with sugar. My husband would like coffee. Thank you." Mr. Garner nodded his agreement.

Martha's thoughts were tumbling one after the other as she made the coffee and tea. Why were Sheryl's parents here?

Martha carried out the hot drinks and set them on the coffee table, and then sat down. She had not made herself a drink as she was too nervous. "Is Sheryl okay?" she asked, suddenly anxious.

"Yes," Mr. Garner said, before taking a sip of coffee. "She's in rehab."

"Rehab?" Martha thought rehab was for drug addicts and alcoholics. "Did Sheryl have a drug problem?"

Mrs. Garner shook her head and dabbed at her eyes with a tissue, but Mr. Garner was the one to speak. "I'll explain everything. We're so sorry you got mixed up in this. Sheryl is a kleptomaniac. Do you know what that is?"

Martha thought for a moment. "Someone who steals things, but can't help it, isn't it?"

"Yes," he said. "We've had trouble with Sheryl stealing for years, and finally had her booked in to see a specialist in this type of thing, but she didn't turn up for her first appointment and we didn't see her again for some time."

"Until she called to tell us she'd been arrested for theft—again," Mrs. Garner said, through her tears.

"Martha, if I may call you Martha?" Mr. Garner asked. Martha nodded, so he continued. "Martha, Sheryl was very upset that the police had arrested you, so she's made a full statement to them that you had nothing to do with it. We've also spoken to the police and they're now aware of the full extent of Sheryl's problem, including the fact that she's always worked alone."

Martha was shocked. The room seemed to spin and she wondered if she were about to faint. The sense of relief was overpowering, so much so, that she didn't know how she'd cope with it.

"So then, it's all straightened out," he added. "The charges against you have been dropped. We'll pay your legal expenses to date." Martha made to speak, but he held up his hand. "We insist. We're quite wealthy people, which makes Sheryl's behavior even harder to understand, although we've always been told that it's a psychiatric disorder. We couldn't have it on our conscience if you paid for a lawyer."

Martha thanked them, but Mr. Garner wouldn't hear of it. "Now, we also don't want you out of pocket with this apartment. Sheryl had paid in advance before her arrest, but we'll pay her share for another month if you want to continue with the apartment, but then you'll have to get the lease transferred out of her name and into yours."

"That's very kind," Martha said, waving their protestations aside, "but I've actually decided to go home. I'm Amish, as Sheryl's likely told you, and I've been on *rumspringa*. I'm going to go home." And Martha meant every word.

Chapter Twenty-Three

Rebecca was thrilled that Martha was home and followed her around like a puppy. Their *daed* was overjoyed, and even their *mudder* was seen smiling when she thought that no one was looking.

Martha, however, was overcome with guilt as she considered that she had abandoned her *familye*. She had rarely visited Esther, who had been ill with morning sickness, or Hannah and the twins during her *rumspringa*.

How could she have stayed away from her *familye* for so long? It made no sense in hindsight. When she had expressed those feelings to Moses, he had explained that this was what *rumspringa* was for, to explore the *Englisch* world, and in most cases, that did happen away from one's *familye*. Well, Martha was home now and would be baptized. She had no intention of leaving the Amish ever again. The very thought made her shudder.

When Martha had first tried on *Englisch* clothes,

she had thought that they had given her a sense of freedom, but now she was glad to be back in Amish clothes. They gave her a sense of security, of belonging, and what's more, no one from now on would ever again look to her outward appearance, but rather, only to what was within.

Martha had fallen back into her routine easily. She felt safe at home, surrounded by the love and care of her *familye* and the community. It contrasted starkly with the isolation she had felt in the *Englisch* world. She from time to time worried about Sarah Beachy. There had been no word from her and Martha wondered what had become of her.

Martha had awoken early, even before her *mudder*, and had put on the *kaffi* to brew. She prepared a big breakfast of fried potatoes, with bacon and eggs, and was buttering the toast just as her *daed*, *mudder*, and Rebecca walked into the kitchen.

"You're up early," her *mudder* said, with clear approval in her voice, and Martha smiled.

"I'll visit Hannah this morning," she said, "if that's okay with you, *Mamm*."

Her *mudder* nodded. "*Jah*, Rebecca can do the laundry. Hannah will be pleased to see you."

Rebecca pulled a face.

After Martha washed up, she walked to Hannah's *haus*, which was on the far side of the Miller property. She waved to Hannah's husband, Noah, as he drove his buggy to the Miller farm to start his day's work as a furniture maker for Martha's *daed*.

The air was pleasant and fresh, and not filled with

car fumes or other disagreeable smells. There was no sound of noise or traffic, only of birds as they went about their own morning duties. The light breeze pushed some wispy clouds along the clear blue sky, and Martha sent up a silent prayer to *Gott* that, finally, she was back where she belonged.

Hannah met Martha at the door, her face beaming, with a *boppli* on each hip. "It's great to see you again," Martha cooed to each *boppli.*

Hannah said jokingly, "What about me?"

They both laughed. "You take Rose, and I'll take Mason."

When Martha hesitated, as both *bopplin* looked alike to her, Hannah bobbed the hip Rose was on in the direction of Martha. Martha took the *boppli*, who held out her little chubby arms to her.

"Oh she's so cute," Martha gushed.

"You'll have a *boppli* soon, Martha."

"Stop teasing me, Hannah." Martha followed Hannah into the living room, where she sat Rose on the rug next to Mason. "Twins must be such hard work."

Hannah smiled. "*Jah*, they are. There are lots and lots of diapers to wash, of course, but the two of them keep each other entertained to some degree. Anyway, would you please make us *kaffi* while I watch them?"

"Sure." Martha stood up. "Don't you want me to help with the laundry, though?"

"Katie, Noah's *mudder*, is coming to do it for me today, but you could help me later in the week."

"Of course I will. I'm so glad to be home."

"Oh, Martha, would you look out the window too,

and make sure Annie and Sophie aren't digging up the yard?"

"Sophie? Did you get another beagle?"

Hannah sighed. "I thought after I had the twins that Annie needed a friend, so Noah brought home a little terrier. Susie Lapp's dog had puppies. Anyway, Annie and Sophie get on well, but Sophie's been quite a bit of trouble. She's always digging holes. Jessie Yoder wanted Sophie, but Mrs. Yoder said the dog would be too much trouble given that they already had Pirate."

Jessie Yoder herself has been quite a bit of trouble, Martha thought, *what with her trying to push Jacob and Esther apart a while back.* She kept that opinion to herself, however, and went to fetch *kaffi* and check on the dogs.

Martha soon returned and handed Hannah a mug of *kaffi*, and reported that both dogs were behaving themselves.

"Now, Martha, tell me all about your *rumspringa*. You're the first girl in the *familye* to go on *rumspringa*. Well, the only one likely to now, as I doubt Rebecca will."

Martha pulled a face. "It was exciting at first, doing something different, but it was very isolating and quite scary really. It was fun to wear the different clothes at first, but I never really got used to them."

"What's television like?"

Martha shrugged. "That was exciting too at first, but a lot of it is all the same. Plus, it's full of violence, so much so that I had to look away from the screen so many times. The *Englisch* are always in a hurry when you see them outside, but when you go into their homes, they are the opposite. They sit and watch television for hours at a time. It was strange, at least to me."

Hannah nodded. "That's what Katie said."

Martha was puzzled. "Katie? You mean Katie Hostetler? Noah's and Moses's *mudder*?"

"*Jah*."

"I didn't know she went on *rumspringa*."

Hannah giggled. "*Jah*, and she even drove a car."

Martha joined in the laughter. "Just as well *Mamm* doesn't know, but I think with you and Esther being married to Hostetler boys, *Mamm* is better about the Hostetler *familye* now."

Hannah sipped her coffee and then propped up Mason, who was lurching precariously to one side to reach a little, wooden toy. "I don't think it was just the accident, with Noah running into our buggy, that made *Mamm* a bit funny over the Hostetlers. She's always seen them as too liberal."

"True." Martha nodded. "But *Datt* is from a more liberal *familye* too, and *Mamm* married him."

Hannah chuckled again. "I didn't say it made sense."

"Oh, Hannah, there's a lot I have to tell you," Martha said, abruptly changing the subject. Martha told Hannah all about her arrest, and all about securing a contract for handmade chocolates.

Hannah listened, totally engrossed by Martha's words, murmuring in dismay, amazement, or delight from time to time, while Martha poured out the whole story. "And I didn't want to tell anyone," Martha concluded, "because I had to keep it from *Mamm,* as she would've made me come straight home, and I didn't want to put the burden of having to keep a secret from *Mamm* on any of you."

"I had no idea," Hannah said. "Well, you sure did have an exciting *rumspringa* after all. That will be something to tell your *kinskinner* in years to come."

Martha laughed, grateful that Hannah was not annoyed with her for keeping the whole secret of her arrest from her. "I don't even have a *boppli* yet, so *kinskinner* are a long way off."

Hannah just raised her eyebrows. "And when you do have *kinner,* how will you run your chocolate business?"

"I've thought about that," Martha said truthfully. "It would be difficult, I'm sure, when they are young, but Mrs. Hostetler has her own successful quilt store."

"*Jah,*" Hannah said, "but her *sohns* are grown up."

Martha nodded. "I might have to employ a *maidel* and train her."

"*Gut* idea, and I'll help you."

Martha beamed widely. "*Denki*, Hannah." She laughed. "Look at us! We have me married and with *kinner* already."

"It won't be long," Hannah said, with a knowing look on her face.

Chapter Twenty-Four

Moses. The name shot through Martha's imagination like a star falling to the earth. He was beautiful, but not in an obvious way. He was the type of man whose winning personality shone through everything he did, illuminating both his face and the world around him. He was tall, although well muscled, and his skin, tanned to a nut-brown, looked particularly radiant on this late summer's afternoon.

It had been two days since Martha had visited Hannah and the twins. It had not been much longer since she had decided not to join the *Englisch* world, deciding instead to stay with Moses and raise little Hostetler *sohns* and *dochders* with the tilled earth beneath their feet, the warm sun above their heads, and their *familyes* surrounding them. Not that Martha had told Moses this just yet. *Moses*. Just the thought of his name made her heart leap.

"Is this box coming with us?"

Martha jumped at the sound of his voice. Since

she had decided to stay Amish, she needed to spend the Saturday cleaning the apartment and donating the few *Englisch* clothes she had bought to local charities. She had roped Moses into the task, promising to buy him ice cream for lunch.

"Mark that one down for donation," replied Martha, wiping a hand against her damp brow. "Thanks again for helping out with the cleaning. I don't know what I would do without you."

"You'd save money on ice cream," he replied, smiling. "That reminds me; it's almost lunch. We can finish up here in an hour or so. How about we walk down the street and get that ice cream you promised me?"

It was a pleasant afternoon. The sun shone down gently upon the pair as they walked along the street toward the river, where the windows of a dozen or so shops glittered behind the rows of trees. Martha chose vanilla from the confectionery store, although Moses was more daring and had a salted caramel cone, before the pair crossed the road and settled by the river, watching small boys push wooden boats away from the shore.

It was weird to think that, in the not so distant future, her *kinner* with Moses might play near a river similar to the one she rested near now. She wondered if she ought to say something to Moses, but with the ice cream running down her face, and the sun starting to burn her nose, she decided to wait a minute or two. Martha liked the silence. She liked that Moses evidently liked the silence too, for he did not say a thing, even after demolishing his ice cream. After fifteen minutes, he turned his handsome smile on her.

"Are you excited to be home?"

Before she could answer his question, the rest of her ice cream slipped from the cone and landed on her dress. She quickly cleaned up the mess, but not quickly enough. Moses let out a roaring laugh.

"It's not funny," said Martha, although she smiled as well. "If I'd been wearing *Englisch* jeans, I suppose I could have washed them, and then donated them to charity. Oh well, no harm done, even though my poor ice cream is no more."

"If I had any left, I'd have shared it with you."

"You eat fast," replied Martha, vaguely. She reached up her hand and wiped a sweep of ice cream off his nose. "Looks like I'm not the only messy one. Hopefully our…"

There was an awkward silence. Martha was just about to mention their *kinner* before she caught herself. Moses had noticed something was amiss. Had he always been so observant? He did know there was something between them well before she did, so perhaps there was no harm in speaking up now. It was the brave thing to do.

"I've been thinking," said Moses, beating her to the punch. "Maybe there was a reason you decided not to become an *Englischer*. At least, I was hoping there was a reason you decided not to become an *Englischer*. I was hoping that reason was me."

The smile lit up Martha's face. "I've been wanting to talk to you, Moses. I should have said something earlier, only it was so pleasant sitting here with you, eating ice cream and watching the little boys play by the river."

"Does that mean…?" Moses took Martha's face in his hands and lightly kissed her on the lips. "Does that mean you love me as much as I love you?"

"More."

"It's not possible." He kissed her again. "My sweet Martha. It's not possible."

"It is," replied Martha, wanting to pinch herself to see if this was real, but not wanting to move away from Moses. "Just now I've been thinking about the *sohns* and *dochders* we will have."

"I've been thinking about that for years," he replied. It felt a little awkward being affectionate in full view of the *Englischers*, but Moses did not let go of Martha's face, and she did not want him to. "And years." He kissed her lightly again, and then he kissed her on the nose. "And years. What have you to say to that, Martha Miller?"

Martha kissed him now. He smelled wonderful, like soap and freshness, and though his hands were rugged from all his farm work over the years, she still loved the weight of them, the warmth of them, pressed against her cheeks. She reached up and brushed the hair out of his eyes, marveling at how bright and wide they were in the summer afternoon light. He truly was the most handsome man she had ever known, and she could not believe her luck that he was hers, all hers, forever more.

Suddenly he let go. Martha forced herself to not look unhappy. She glanced down at her hands just as he took them in his own.

"Will you marry me?" he asked.

"Yes," she replied, without hesitation.

The boys' mother had joined them by the river, and she cheered on hearing the proposal. It made Martha blush, and Moses grin, and the small boys roll their eyes and pick up their boats, dragging their mother away from the young couple. Martha felt warm all over at the notion of embarrassing her own *sohns* one day.

"Who would have thought it?" said Moses. "Three Miller *schweschders* married to three Hostetler *bruders*. I wonder if our parents ever considered this a possibility when we were all born?"

"I wonder," replied Martha. She stood now, keeping her hands entwined with Moses's. "We should go and finish packing up all my stuff. I'm ready to put this part of my life behind me now that I've found you. It's been an experience, though somehow not a terrible one, and it's led me to you."

"For that," he replied, "I will always be thankful." He lifted up her hands and kissed each one. It made Martha smile more than she could have ever thought possible.

"You know," she replied, "I never answered your question."

"And what question was that, my little love?"

"Yes." A shy smile swept over her face as they walked hand in hand back to her apartment, where boxes upon boxes awaited them both. "I am excited to be home. After all, I have come home to you."

* * * * *

WE HOPE YOU ENJOYED
THIS BOOK FROM

LOVE INSPIRED
INSPIRATIONAL ROMANCE

Uplifting stories of faith, forgiveness and hope.

Fall in love with stories where faith helps
guide you through life's challenges, and discover
the promise of a new beginning.

6 NEW BOOKS AVAILABLE EVERY MONTH!

SPECIAL EXCERPT FROM

🍃

LOVE INSPIRED
INSPIRATIONAL ROMANCE

*Intent on reopening a local bed-and-breakfast,
Addie Ricci sank all her savings into the project—and
now the single mother's in over her head. But her high
school sweetheart's back in town and happy to lend a
hand. Will Addie's long-kept secret stand in the way of
their second chance?*

*Read on for a sneak preview of
Her Hidden Hope by Jill Lynn,
part of her Colorado Grooms miniseries.*

Addie kept monopolizing Evan's time. First at the B and B—though she could hardly blame herself for that. He was the one who'd insisted on helping her out. And now again at church. Surely he had better places to be than with her.

"Do you need to go?" she asked Evan. "Sorry I kept you so long."

"I'm not in a rush. I might pop out to Wilder Ranch for lunch with Jace and Mackenzie. After that I have to…" Evan groaned.

"Run into a burning building? Perform brain surgery? Teach a sewing class?"

Humor momentarily flashed across his features. "Go to a meeting for Old Westbend Weekend."

What? So much for some Evan-free time to pull herself back together. "I'm going to that, but I didn't realize you were. The B and B is one of the sponsors for the weekend." Addie had used her entire limited advertising budget for the three-day event.

"I thought my brother might block for me today. Instead he totally kicked me under the bus as it roared by. He caught Bill's attention and volunteered me for the hero thing." The pure torment on Evan's face was almost comical. "I want to back out of it, but Bill played the 'it's for the kids' card, and now I think I'm trapped."

"Look, Mommy!" Sawyer ran over to them. A grubby, slimy—and very dead—worm rested in the palm of his hand.

"Ew."

At her disgust, Sawyer showed the prize to Evan. "Good find. He looks like he's dead, though, so you'd better give him a proper burial."

"Yeah!" Sawyer hurried over to the patch of dirt. He plopped the worm onto the sidewalk and told it to "stay" just like he would Belay. That made both of them laugh. Then he used one of the sticks as a shovel and began digging a hole.

"He's like a cat, always bringing me dead animals as gifts. I'm surprised he doesn't leave them for me on the doorstep."

Evan chuckled while waving toward the parking lot. She turned to see his brother and Mackenzie walking to their vehicle.

"Do you guys want to come out to Wilder Ranch for lunch? I'm sure they wouldn't mind two more. It's a happy sort of chaos there with all of the kids."

Addie's heart constricted at the offer. No doubt Sawyer would love it. She wanted exactly what Evan was offering, but all of that was off-limits for her. She couldn't allow herself any more access into Evan's world or vice versa.

"We can't, but thanks. I've got to get Sawyer down for a nap." Addie wasn't about to attempt attending a meeting with a tired Sawyer, and she didn't have anywhere else in town for him to go.

Evan's face morphed from relaxed to taut, but he didn't press further. "Right. Okay. I guess I'll see you later then." After saying goodbye to Sawyer, he caught up with Jace and Mackenzie in the parking lot.

A momentary flash of loss ached in Addie's chest. A few days in Evan's presence and he was already showing her how different things could have been. It was like there was a life out there that she'd missed by taking the wrong path. It was shiny and warm and so, so out of reach.

And the worst of it was, until Evan, she hadn't realized just how much she was missing.

Don't miss
Her Hidden Hope *by Jill Lynn,*
available May 2020 wherever
Love Inspired books and ebooks are sold.

LoveInspired.com

SPECIAL EXCERPT FROM

LOVE INSPIRED SUSPENSE
INSPIRATIONAL ROMANCE

Someone is trying to force her off her land, and her only hope lies in the secret father of her child, who has come back home to sell his property.

Read on for a sneak preview of
Dangerous Amish Inheritance *by Debby Giusti,*
available April 2020 from Love Inspired Suspense.

Ruthie Eicher awoke with a start. She blinked in the darkness and touched the opposite side of the double bed, where her husband had slept. Two months since the tragic accident and she was not yet used to his absence.

Finding the far side of the bed empty and the sheets cold, she dropped her feet to the floor and hurried into the children's room. Even without lighting the oil lamp, she knew from the steady draw of their breaths that nine-year-old Simon and six-year-old Andrew were sound asleep.

Movement near the outbuildings caught her eye. She held her breath and stared for a long moment.

Narrowing her gaze, she leaned forward, and her heart raced as a flame licked the air.

She shook Simon. "The woodpile. On fire. I need help."

He rubbed his eyes.

"Hurry, Simon."

Leaving him to crawl from bed, she raced downstairs, almost tripping, her heart pounding as she knew all too well how quickly the fire could spread. She ran through the kitchen, grabbed the back doorknob and groaned as her fingers struggled with the lock.

"No!" she moaned, and coaxed her fumbling hands to work. The lock disengaged. She threw open the door and ran across the porch and down the steps.

A noise sounded behind her. She glanced over her shoulder, expecting Simon. Instead she saw a large, darkly dressed figure. Something struck the side of her head. She gasped with pain, dropped the bucket and stumbled toward the house.

He grabbed her shoulder and threw her to the ground. She cried out, struggled to her knees and started to crawl away. He kicked her side. She groaned and tried to stand. He tangled his fingers through her hair and pulled her to her feet.

The man's lips touched her ear. "Didn't you read my notes? You don't belong here." His rancid breath soured the air. "Leave before something happens to you and your children."

Don't miss
Dangerous Amish Inheritance *by Debby Giusti,*
available April 2020 wherever
Love Inspired Suspense books and ebooks are sold.

LoveInspired.com

LISEXP0420

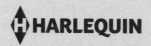

HARLEQUIN

Heartfelt or suspenseful, inspiring or passionate, Harlequin has your happily-ever-after.

With new books published
every month, you are sure to find the
satisfying escape you know you deserve.